Wish You Were Here

Catherine Clark

HARPERTEEN

An Imprint of HarperCollins*Publishers*

HarperTeen is an imprint of HarperCollins Publishers.

Library of Congress Cataloging-in-Publication Data
Clark, Catherine, 1962-
    Wish you were here / Catherine Clark. — 1st ed.
        p.   cm.
    Summary: On a free-wheeling bus tour of the West with assorted
family members, senior citizens galore, and one boy her age, sixteen-
year-old Ariel writes postcards to her maybe-boyfriend and others
while trying to cope with the effects of her parents' divorce.
    ISBN 978-0-06-055983-0 (trade bdg.)
    ISBN 978-0-06-055984-7 (lib. bdg.)
    [1. Bus travel—Fiction.   2. Vacations—Fiction.   3. Family life—
Fiction.   4. Divorce—Fiction.   5. Postcards—Fiction.   6. West
(U.S.)—Fiction.]   I. Title.
PZ7.C5412Wis   2008   2007033299
[Fic]—dc22

Typography by Ray Shappell

1 2 3 4 5 6 7 8 9 10

First Edition

HELLO
my name is

For Ted,
King of the road

Thanks to my wonderfulovely editor, Amanda Maciel,
and to my fantasterrific agent, Jill Grinberg.
Thanks to Cady for letting me write.
And to Ted for taking care of Cady so I could.
Thanks to my writers group.
This is starting to sound like that Alanis Morissette song.
Thanks to the Loft for the studios to write in.
To Peace Coffee, and other coffees of the Twin Cities.
To the postcard writers and photographers of America.
To my friends for always picking out the bizarre ones
and sending them to me.
With apologies to everyone in South Dakota for taking liberties
with their landmarks. If I got anything wrong and made unforgivable
mistakes, remember I'm just a girl from Massachusetts,
which could fit inside South Dakota and still leave room for the
rest of New England, and then some. (Don't quote me on this.)

XO
CC

Wish You Were Here

Chapter One

I'm on my bike, bringing my semi-new, semi-boyfriend, Dylan, a bag of Skittles, and the candies are rattling in my backpack like those little fake rocks my mother has in her miniature Zen serenity desk fountain.

I picture getting to Dylan's house and spelling out his name, or my name, with the Skittles, or encircling our initials in a heart shape with a giant + in the middle. Then we'll frolic on his bedroom floor in the Skittles as part of our long, romantic good-bye.

I have a very active fantasy life. Dylan's not the frolic-in-Skittles type of person, and probably neither am I.

I am, however, addicted to eating Skittles, so I can't really see why I'm giving away an entire bag. Maybe it's because now I'm addicted to Dylan instead, or maybe it's because I had six bags stashed in my desk drawer, so it was very handy and didn't require another trip to Target, where I've already been five times in the last two days getting stuff for our summer trip.

"Ariel, this isn't the only Target in the world," my mother keeps saying. "You realize there will be *stores* where we're going." But I don't trust her, because she won't even tell us where it is we're going. And besides, what does she know about being addicted to Skittles?

When I get to his house, Dylan opens the front door. He has sandy cinnamon-colored hair that's cut short, and he has sideburns that make him look older than seventeen.

His face lights up when he sees me, like it always used to when I walked into Spanish when we were in the ninth grade, back when we were friends, before we were whatever we are now. His light blue eyes have brown flecks, which makes them hard not to gaze into. I've tried. Like, all through ninth grade I tried.

I worry that he's only smiling because he sees me holding the Skittles, so I hand the bag to him, but he doesn't seem overly excited by them, and he keeps looking happy to see me. Which is sweet. Like Skittles-candy-sweet. Addictive, for sure.

"Hey, you," he says. "What's up?"

"Not much. Just packing. For the tenth time."

"Right. Me too," he says. "You want to come in? Come on in." He opens the door wide. When I walk past him, he does this cute little thing where he pinches my waist, only I don't have much waist, so he pinches hip bone instead. I still can't believe he actually does things like this to me.

I'm not saying that I'm an ultra-thin girl. I just don't seem to keep much weight on these days. I think partly it's because I'm a runner, and because my parents just had this ugly breakup, and because my mother plans to drag me all over the country this summer, and I'm worried how that's going to turn out. I mean, there are the normal worries, on that front, and then there are the new worries: like, what if Dylan has this amazingly exciting summer in Wyoming and meets someone new and falls in love with her? While I'm stuck on a road trip with my mom and sister? And did I mention that after our road trip, we're spending two weeks at my grandparents' house?

Of course, I could be home all summer, pathetically waiting for Dylan's return, which would not be any better, let's face it. If he's going to be gone for two months, then I might as well ditch too. I just wish we weren't going to be so far apart, for so long.

I'm barely over the shock of the fact that we hooked up at our school's Spring Fling. There I was, with two weeks left of school, just getting over the thrill of our track team coming in second in state, me coming in third in the 1600. (It was exciting, at least at the time, because nobody thought I was going to place that high, not even me.) Sarah and I were hanging out, wondering if there was much flinging to be done, really, when she left to talk to her physics teacher and I ran into Dylan, who throws the javelin. So we started talking about track, then about other stuff too, laughing and dancing.

We kept looking at each other and then we started holding hands. We even left the dance together, which was huge, and he was going to drive me home, because we live close to each other, but I had to go back inside because of course I forgot my cute little gold shoulder wrap thingie, and when I left again, there was Dylan, right where I left him, and I thought, *What is happening? Is he actually waiting for me? No one ever waits for me.*

I'm with Perfect Dylan now. It's the best thing that's happened to me during what has been a very imperfect year.

Now, two weeks later, it's the beginning of summer and he's leaving and I'm leaving and that is all so imperfect that I would promise to give up Skittles if it would change anything. But it won't, so what's the point in suffering? You don't go on hunger strikes, or

Skittles strikes, for just *anything*.

We walk into Dylan's room and I flop onto his Green Bay Packers beanbag chair by the door, which nearly swallows me. I struggle to sit up.

"You know what?" I say. "I need your address at camp."

"I already gave it to you," Dylan says.

"I know, but I lost it," I say. Actually I didn't. In fact I have it, and I've also already memorized it. Probably it's a bad sign to be lying this early in our relationship.

"Oh. Well, okay," Dylan says, and he writes down the address again on a scrap of paper that turns out to be a receipt from the Hollister store at the mall, which I will cherish even though it's all inventory numbers except for the words "s/s tee." I just want more of his handwriting, more things to remind me that he exists when the tires are rolling down the pavement and I'm staring at the back of my little sister's head, because of course she'll insist on sitting up front at least some of the time.

"Do you think you'll come home for a visit?" I ask.

"Nope. Not a chance." He slides into the beanbag chair beside me and we snuggle, because there's no other option when two people are in a beanbag chair, which is probably why they were invented.

"Are you sure you're not going to have email all summer?" I lean against his shoulder, the rock-hard-javelin-pitching shoulder.

"Not unless they really changed things from last year," he says.

"My mom's insisting that we give up email and cell phones, too. We're supposed to just enjoy each other." I laugh.

She says my cell phone has become a "crutch," and that she wants some time alone for us as a family, so she doesn't want anyone to be able to reach me. In other words, she doesn't want Dad to reach me.

He's not included anymore in the "time as a family" time.

It's ironic because my dad was the one who was into taking summer trips—my mom went along reluctantly, after my dad spent hours planning them. Now we're going, she has zero planned, and my dad will be at home, living with Grandma and Grandpa Flack, where he had to move after Mom kicked him out. All Grandma Flack could do was joke that at least she'd kept his room the same for the past twenty years.

"My mom wants me to focus on 'the now,' to experience the journey," I tell Dylan.

He raises his eyebrows. He's met my mom, and knows she's the type of person who can spend time canvassing the neighborhood to get everyone to vote to legalize hemp.

In other words, crazy, though she says that's not a nice word, because it's an illness, which she'd know because she's a counselor, and I should use the term "mentally ill" instead—but only when I'm talking about other people, and not her.

"So this sucks. You can't call, and I can't email you," Dylan says, as he keeps shooting a Nerf ball into the air and catching it again.

"Sometimes I might be able to, I guess," I say. "It depends on where we stop, you know?"

"You know what would be cool? If you ended up coming close to camp."

"That would be cool," I agree. "Impossible, but cool. It doesn't sound like we're going west, but you never know. Maybe I'll take over the driving. Carjack the Jetta."

Dylan laughs. "Is that possible when you're actually in the car already?"

"We'll see." I'm a little worried about Mom being able to pull off her so-called itinerary. She doesn't seem to have much planned at all.

I've seen no maps, no AAA TripTiks. She keeps saying how we'll let the winds take us and the stars can light our way and other feel-good, schmaltzy stuff like that.

I think it's because secretly she is a horrible navigator, and she's going to hand me that job—but no map—as soon as we hit the road. I'll have to look for stars to guide us, and I'll regret that I never paid attention to that astronomy mini class, and wish that the wind would quickly blow us home *Wizard of Oz* style.

I look at my watch and see that it's almost time for me to go home and see Grandma Flack, who's coming over to pick up my cat, Gloves. She's taking care of Gloves for the next few weeks while we're away.

But I don't want to leave Dylan, not yet. I want to stay here. I want to fold up into a suitcase with a big label that says, "Dylan Meander." Not as in "Property of," because that would be tacky and also it would set women's rights back a thousand years, but just so they know where to deliver me when the suitcase gets to his dude-ranch-style camp, which cabin they should drop me at.

Is that so wrong?

I guess.

I try to get up from the beanbag chair, but I keep slipping. Dylan tries to help me up, but then he sinks down beside me and puts his arms around my waist because I'm starting to sort of cry a little, which I hate.

I loathe saying good-bye at the end of the school year. I just do. Even to people who write in my yearbook when I don't even really know them all that well and they write really, really stupid things. I still feel myself getting choked up because it's so nice that they want to write *some*thing, and I love them.

Then they hand me their yearbooks and I hate them, because I don't know them well enough to write anything, and I, unlike them, can't come up with something on the spot. I'm the worst spontaneous writer in the world. I need Time, capital T, to think of what I want to say and how to say it best.

But then this year, now that I think about it, not as many people asked me to sign their yearbooks, which should have been a relief, but it wasn't. Because although I used to be fairly popular, ever since the thing with my dad being in trouble, some people dropped me. I'm not on the A list anymore. I'm somewhere between B and C, or maybe C and D. Unlike my bra size.

My mind is wandering. It's because I don't want to leave, because leaving is like stepping off a giant precipice into the scary canyon known as Summer. You don't abandon your first actual sort-of boyfriend. You just don't. Right? That's one of the rules. But I think about poor Gloves being taken away, without me there for comfort.

"I have to go," I say.

"Okay," Dylan says.

"So, bye."

"Bye."

We don't move.

"You first," he says.

"No, you," I say.

We look at each other and smile, and then he kisses me, and I kiss him. This should be such a romantic good-bye that I wait for that melting feeling, but it doesn't happen.

I tell myself that's because it's only June, which is not the melting season, and we've been dating only two weeks. In August, when we both get home from our summer thingies and look at each other, we'll melt like a couple of Skittles left in the car on a hot day with the windows up.

For now, Dylan is snuggling with me and doing these moves that I'm not really sure I understand. But okay, I'm new at this, and maybe he is, too. I don't feel anything except awkward, and sort of tense, and worried that his mom's going to walk in on us.

I contemplate fake-melting, until I realize that although I thought he was sort of ravishing me, he was actually trying to get his cell phone off the desk because it's buzzing to tell him he has a text message. I can't help feeling that although I kind of love him, right now I kind of hate him.

"Are you really going to read that now?" I ask.

"No, no, I just thought—maybe it was the camp," he says.

"Right. What's it called again?" I ask, hating that he's so excited about leaving for the place.

"Camp Far-a-Way," he says.

"Ha-ha."

"No, really. It is."

On the way home I drop my first perfectly written, preplanned postcard in the mailbox.

The cows are the real stars of the Wisconsin State Fair!

Hey—

I know we only saw each other like 10 minutes ago, but I wanted you to have something to read when you got to camp.

Me: preparing myself for life on the road with Mom and Zena.

You: getting ready for awesome summer on a ranch.

This is Not Fair.

Neither is it a state fair.

Miss you already.

Hurry back,

Ariel

Do not write below this line. Space reserved for U.S. Postal Service.

Chapter Two

I go home and Grandma Flack isn't there yet, so I review my mother's list of what I should pack, like the kind they give you when you go away to summer camp, which is where I should be going, with Dylan.

Camp Far-a-Way. Is he serious?

Shirts: 4
Pants: 3
Shorts: 4

I revised her list. Slightly. She doesn't seem to realize this road trip is two weeks long, and then we're going to Grandma and Grandpa Timmons's house, and even though I can do laundry there, do I really want to wear the same four shirts all summer?

Shirts: 23 (roughly)
Jeans: 7
Shorts: 10
Running shorts: 8
Running shirts: 8

Socks:	**Lots**
Shoes:	**16 (That's eight pairs, so it's really not as bad as it sounds. I have this sort of obsession with vintage running shoes, so in addition to my new favorites for running, of which I have two pairs, I also have five pairs for not running, and one pair of flip-flops.)**
Books:	**7**
Notebooks:	**3**
Large bags of Skittles:	**5**

My suitcase won't close without major amounts of sitting on it and smashing it.

Mom catches me jumping up and down on my suitcase and wants to know what's inside that's making it so hard to fasten and why I have an extra duffel on the side, like an order of French fries.

"It's all my running stuff," I say. "I have to bring clothes for every climate."

"Okay, whatever, Ariel," she says, looking frazzled. Her graying dirty blond hair is flying out in several directions, as if she's been caught in a hurricane—that's what happens to it when she doesn't use her blow-dryer and product. She and Zena have the same curly, wavy, unruly hair. Me, I have Dad's hair: dark brown, straight, ruly.

"But you definitely won't be able to buy anything new on our trip. We simply don't have room," she says.

"We don't? But it's only the three of us, and we always had room before," I argue.

"This isn't *before*," she says. "This is after." She pauses as if she wants to remember those lines for a chapter title for one of her new books. She forces a small smile. "Anyway, the road trip is only two weeks. How much could you possibly need to wear?"

"Maybe I like to change my clothes more often than you do." I check out her shirt, which looks as rumpled as her hair. "Didn't you work today?"

"Yes, but only in the morning," she says. "So, remember: no CDs, no DVDs, no cell phone—"

"Why is that exactly, again?" I ask.

"We're focusing on us. We're keeping it realsimple," my mother says. This is one of her buzzwords. "Realsimple." As if it's one word. She and everyone in her family have this thing for inventing words, mashing them together until they fit, the way you do with jigsaw puzzle pieces.

I'm surprised she didn't give us compound names when we were born.

Instead, it was Dad's idea to just close his eyes and flip to a page in the baby name book and point. Once a gambler, always a gambler, I guess.

The section they apparently kept landing on was called STRANGE NAMES, or NAMES TO EMBARRASS YOUR DAUGHTERS FOREVER.

Never mind that the movie *The Little Mermaid* was something everyone had memorized by the time I got to preschool, and I had to explain that no, I didn't have a tail. I got so many *Little Mermaid* gifts that for five years my room had an aquarium theme.

The only thing worse than being named after a cartoon character, in my opinion, is not being named after her, or anyone. Just being a random choice that your parents made with their eyes closed.

My twelve-year-old-sister, Zena, thinks having an unusual name is cool. But then, she also thinks that reading *Us* and *People* should count toward her Summer Literature List requirement. She loves signing things with her initials, because nobody else has them. ZIF. Zena Iris Flack.

She'd better hope that Mom doesn't want us to change our names back to her maiden name, which is Timmons, because her initials will then be ZIT. Monograms will be a problem. (My middle name is Frances, so I'll just go from AFF to AFT.)

Zena comes upon me and Mom arguing about the lack of email and phone, and says, "Just relax, A. So we won't have email, so what?"

We have this silly habit of calling each other "A" and "Z," because Dad always used to refer to us as "A to Z."

"Z, it's a big deal. I need to stay in touch with people."

"It won't be forever. What, are you worried Dylan's going to forget you or something?" she scoffs.

"No, of course not," I bluff.

But of course I am. So, the thing is, I'm going to write to him whenever I can. And send postcards of all the tacky places we go. My friend Sarah and I came up with the plan: she, because she doesn't want me to be out of touch for weeks; me, because I don't want anyone to forget me. Not Sarah, not Dylan, not even Gloves.

The doorbell chimes, and it's Grandma Flack. "Tamara. A pleasure," she says to Mom. "All set for the trip?"

"Almost." Without another word, Mom runs up the stairs to pack, leaving us to visit on our own. We always used to get along fine. Now it's weird and strained sometimes, like my grandma is guilty of something because she took in Dad, but it's not like I wouldn't want her to do that. Everything just feels extremely formal.

We shrug and look at one another as Mom thunders off. "She's busy," I say.

"Oh, sure." Our grandmother nods.

I wonder why my dad didn't come over with her to say good-bye, but then I remember that the last time he and Mom saw each other was not pretty. Nothing was hurled except insults, but still. It's not something you want to see twice in your lifetime, never mind thirty times.

My grandmother gives me an envelope. "This is from your dad," she says, and inside is a hundred-dollar bill, which I have to wonder how he could afford and if it's really from him, or really from her, trying to cover for him. "He wants you to have a great time on the trip, so here's some 'mad money,' I think he called it."

Mad money. Interesting choice of words. It's a good thing Mom isn't here, because she'd be furious at Dad for handing out money when he's supposedly bankrupt. "What about Zena?" I ask. "Is she getting some angry cash for the trip, too?"

Grandma Flack laughs. "No, she can share yours," she says. "She's not responsible enough yet."

Neither is Dad, I think. Not to sound pop-psycho like my mother, but I don't necessarily know if age has anything to do with how responsible a person is. Unlike my mom, I keep my opinion to myself. But I also get this weird feeling in the pit of my stomach when I wonder why my dad isn't on the scene to say good-bye.

"So . . . why didn't he come by to see us before we left, too?" I ask.

"I think we both know why," she replies. And although it's true, that the last bunch of visits have been weird, and I don't know how to feel around him now, and sometimes he just makes me nervous . . . I think he should keep attempting them.

"Um, I'll go try to find Gloves," I say.

I hunt around the house, in all of Gloves's favorite hiding places. Speaking of hiding, sometimes I think Mom's taking us on this trip just to keep us from staying in touch with Dad. In fact, maybe she's planning to stash us in some new town where he can't find us. Not that anything he did was so wrong, unless of course you prefer not having your life's savings, your college fund, and your house, even, stolen out from under you and used to bet on slots, cards, horses, and God knows what else.

The whole blackjack craze. Dad got swept up in it. Like, literally, off his chair and onto the floor and into the dustbin of history. From there it was an easy trip to the horse track, etc.

There aren't a lot of Flacks in town, so it wasn't something you could pretend was happening to someone else. At all.

Grandpa Flack told me that at his bar, there was a new game invented called "Flackjack," which was a version of blackjack that involved stealing from the kitty when the other players weren't looking. He didn't find it amusing and never went back to the place where he'd been a regular for twenty years.

Dad did things like this. He ruined things, kind of like when you throw a rock into a lake and it not only sends out ripples, it also lands on a fish and kills it.

That's us. The dead fish.

I spot Gloves lying under my comforter, on the corner of the bed near the window, basking in the sun. She shouldn't be a Wisconsin cat. She doesn't have thick enough fur. I scoop her overheated body up and give her a few kisses, right on the white patch over her eyes. "Don't worry, G. You'll be fine," I tell her. "Things are going to be weird, but I'll be home soon. If you get lonely, Dad will be there."

He's the one who helped me pick out Gloves seven years ago at the Humane Society. He was also the one who suggested we take her back after she cried nonstop on the way home.

I find Grandma in the kitchen, visiting with Zena and picking up the bags of cat food and other Gloves supplies that I packed that morning. "Hey, Dad's not in Las Vegas or something, is he?" I ask her.

"No, of course not. Why would he be in Vegas?" she asks, as if that's the most illogical thing I've ever said. "He's done with gambling," she says. "You know that."

"Right," I say. He's definitely promised to change, and I haven't noticed anything suspicious lately, but it hasn't been that long, either.

"So, I got you something, too." She gives me a thin plastic sleeve of stamps. Two books of regular first-class stamps, a few sheets of postcard stamps, plus some plain white postcards, already stamped.

We've always had this weird, slightly psychic connection. "How did you know?" I ask.

"Know what?" she says.

"That I need stamps," I say.

"Please. That bit about not bringing a computer along and springing for wireless, or giving you a phone? Ridiculous." She snorts. "Penny wise, pound foolish." She's always saying this about my mother, which probably isn't that cool a quality in a mother-in-law. Or an ex-mother-in-law, which I guess would be a mother outlaw.

I keep looking at her and wondering whether it was her who made Dad the way he is, or whether it was us, or whether it wouldn't have mattered who he was born or married to—maybe he was wired from the womb to be a gambling addict.

"I wouldn't last a day without emailing my friends," she says.

"Yeah. Maybe I won't, either," I say. A day sounds about right, give or take a few hours.

"Also, it wouldn't kill you to keep in touch with your father while you're away," she says. "Think about it."

It wouldn't kill me to keep in touch, but it might hurt, sort of like getting blood drawn. He lied about so many things that I still haven't really been able to forgive him for, even though at one point I really did decide that he was a good person at heart, a good person with a really big problem. And forgiveness is what we need here.

But so far the only one who seems really open to that idea is Zena, who says he can't help himself. I guess I understand that, but I don't really think it's an excuse.

Mom and I aren't budging, but for different reasons.

She's mad about the money, about his lying to her, about how he let everything spiral out of control before he told her what was going on.

And I'm angry about all that too, but I'm also mad about the reputation factor. First it hit the newspaper that he'd embezzled money from the motor vehicle department—which, face it, nobody loves anyway—to finance his gambling habit, after he'd spent all of our money. Then it was on the TV news, and they showed a picture of our house, which is pretty nice, I guess, which looks really bad if someone is stealing government money. Then the Fox News I-Team investigator came to the door and I opened it, not realizing who it was, and the reporter shoved a microphone in my face, and that night it was all over TV, with me saying, "No comment."

When I got to school the next day, it seemed like everyone stood back from me, or whispered, or walked by me saying, "No comment," and laughing.

A few days later, there was this big winter formal, and Sarah told me I had to still go, because I'd already bought a dress and because you can't just give in when people try to shun you. Mom told me to go, and for some reason I thought I might cut loose and have fun. At the dance I was trying to be brave, so I asked Tony Miller if he wanted to dance. He said, "No comment," and grinned at me, as if it were a hilarious and original thing to say. His friends started laughing, so I went into the bathroom to get away from them.

Unfortunately, I happened to be washing my hands at the same time a group of cheerleaders were fixing their hair and makeup.

Sherry Hansen said, "God, Ariel, that's so awful that now you're, like, bankrupt; that must be *so* hard," and another cheerleader tried to hand me a Kleenex, the whole time digging for sordid details, only being nice so they could get the scoop.

I went outside to get some fresh air after that, and Keith Johnson, who was standing there illicitly smoking, tried to commiserate with me by sharing stories of his brother in drug rehab. "Oh yeah, you have it so hard. That's *nothing*. It's *nothing* until he calls you from jail, or beat up in an alley."

"Well, thanks, Keith. I'll look forward to that," I told him. "Thanks *so* much."

Then after I stomped off in my heels, I felt really bad, because he really was worse off than me.

I spent winter break in hibernation. Going back to school afterward was one of the best and hardest things I've ever done. Fortunately there was a scandal involving a football coach and one of the previously mentioned cheerleaders, so everyone moved on to that and forgot about me and my problems. But not before I'd slipped down a few rungs on the cool ladder, rungs I've not managed to climb back up yet. I doubt I ever will. I've got zero upper-body strength. Zero upper body, actually.

I have these really angry thoughts and memories as I'm standing there smiling at my grandmother and clutching Gloves to me. I feel like such a hypocrite. How can I talk to her and make nice about this situation, but how can I not? It's so awkward that sometimes I'd rather jump out the window than feel it all over again. It's getting old and stale, like what happens to Gummi Bears if you open the bag and don't finish them.

I start crying while I say good-bye to Gloves. I've got my nose buried in her black fur, and the thought of abandoning her for four weeks is too much. I rub her white paws. I think about how Gloves will be at Grandma and Grandpa Flack's house, and how Dad will be there, too, and how we won't be, and I keep crying. I'm overreacting and I know it, but I can't stop.

"Pull it together already," Zena says to me. "It's only four weeks. And it's only a cat."

I glare at her through my tears as she hugs Grandma good-bye and then runs upstairs. "Thanks for the sympathy!" I yell after her. She should know that Gloves is not "only a cat." She's my confidante. Unlike my little sister.

"You can always write to her," my grandmother says as she hugs me. "While you're at it, write to me, too. It's going to be as boring as your mother's mac and cheese around here without you." My mother is notorious for her bland cooking, heavy on the dairy. She once made a soup that my dad called "cream of cream."

I laugh. "Okay, I will. I promise."

"Promise?"

"Right," I say, and she kisses my forehead, then gently lifts Gloves out of my arms.

As Gloves is being whisked away in a Pet Porter and plaintively meowing, the phone rings and it's Dylan. I'm glad for the interruption. He thanks me for the Skittles, which strikes me as weird. Of course, he is perfect, so knowing that it would mean a lot to me is probably why he felt compelled to, because we're in sync.

Then he says something not-so-perfect. "You know, whatever happens this summer . . . it's cool, right?" he asks.

"What do you mean?" I ask.

"We sort of have this thing, or we, like, had this thing at the end of the year, and that's cool," Dylan says, "but we won't see each other for ten weeks, and you never know, you might meet someone on your trip."

"Yeah," I say slowly, kind of like a dying breath. *What is he talking about?*

"All I'm saying is that it's going to be a long summer, so . . . don't sweat it if something else comes up," Dylan says.

I'm a little slow at this, but it dawns on me that he's giving me license to see someone else, which probably means that's what he wants to do. "Dylan, what are you saying?"

"Hey, lighten up. It's no big deal, I just want you to have a good time. You know what they say about road trips."

"No." *That they kill your relationship? Before you even leave town?*

"Like, whatever happens on the road stays on the road. Or whatever." He gives an embarrassed laugh.

"I thought that was Las Vegas." *Why does that city keep coming up?*

"Really? Huh."

"Dylan. I'm going on a road trip with my sister and my mom. Do you seriously think I'm going to do anything fun?" I ask. "I'll be in every night by, like, eight. Watching TV in some motel and fighting about what shows to watch."

We say good-bye and I hang up, and then I have that love him/hate him feeling again. I take that slip of paper with his address out of my pocket and stare at it. I have this urge to crumple it and throw it in the kitchen trash, but I don't.

Anyway, even if I did, I've already memorized it, so it would be all for show, and nobody else is around.

Riding the range in the San Juan Mountains of Colorado.
Fun for the whole family!

Hey Dylan,
Have fun becoming a cowboy.
   Hope this will spur you on.
   Okay, not funny.
   (I saved this from a trip 2 years ago.)
See you in 10 weeks!!!
Ariel

P.S. Why Wyoming? Couldn't you pick
somewhere closer?

l...ll...ll..l.lll...dl...ll...ll...l.l..l.ll.l..l.h....l.ll

Chapter Three

We leave at five a.m. in our old diesel VW Jetta. My mother drives as if her hair is on fire. As if we are seeing all fifty states—today. Before lunch.

We hit a bird at about six a.m. and all she, birdwatcher in a former life with my dad the full-time gambler and part-time ornithologist, can say is, "What kind of bird *was* that?"

"Pigeon," I say, because I want to believe that only the ugly birds get hit by runaway middle-aged drivers.

Mom slams on the brakes and pulls into the emergency lane to stop completely; then she backs up, weaving a little. A giant truck lays onto the horn and veers into the left lane to avoid hitting us.

"You are going to kill us!" I say. "You realize that?"

"Just hold your horses," she says, and she climbs out, searching for the wounded bird.

Zena and I watch her wander up the side of the highway, in the dawn. "She has this urge to save helpless things," I comment.

"Helpless *dead* things," Zena corrects me.

"I didn't see anything," Mom says as she climbs back into the car. "Maybe I didn't kill it. Maybe the bird just bounced off the windshield and flew away."

"Mm," I say.

"Maybe," says Zena.

Highly doubtful, I think. This seems like a really bad start to our trip.

We all settle back into our seats and prepare for the next roadkill experience.

Sometimes Mom floors it up to eighty-five; then she'll get distracted and slow to sixty. I can't stand someone who's that inconsistent. If I can keep pace when I'm running and I don't even have a speedometer, then why can't she?

"Mother. There is such a thing as cruise control," I tell her.

She glares at me, then laughs at herself, then switches it on, then off, because she can't decide which she likes better: scaring others or saving gas money. She's seeming a little scattered and out of control this morning, and I wonder why, and want to suggest to her that it's because she's feeling cut off with this no email/no cell phone rule, which should immediately be retracted.

I'm supposed to be allowed to share the driving, but Mom isn't budging from the wheel, and we're not allowed to stop until we nearly run out of gas. This is very unlike my mom, who is always very safe and doesn't like to leave things to chance.

Mom's not the risk-taker; Dad is. She's changing on me, or something, right in the middle of I-94. Maybe she's been reading her own books, especially those chapters about reinventing yourself in *Change Your Wife, Change Your Life*?

Yes, I've read her three books. No, they haven't changed *me*.

* ● *

I spend the first three hours of the drive doing some very significant highway dreaming.

I see: me and Dylan kissing good-bye in his room, which was very hot. Not the room, but the kiss. I wonder if he is thinking about it, too, if he's on the plane, staring out the window, thinking of me. Maybe the plane is overhead right now. At this second. I gaze up through the sunroof, but it's mottled because there was a light, spitting rain overnight that left lots of drecky polka dots.

I see: Dylan and me dancing at a party, but instead of us being on the edge of the dance floor, like we were at Spring Fling, we're in the middle or maybe toward the stage, because we've just been crowned fall Homecoming King and Queen, because everyone's forgotten my dad's a heel and I'm popular again, even more so because I'm with Dylan now, and there's a spotlight on us as we have this big, hot kiss.

Then the daydreaming stops because I actually fall asleep and do some very real dreaming, but unfortunately I can't control these and so it's not about Dylan; it's about showing up to take an exam and having forgotten to wear any clothes and everyone laughing at me as I try to shield myself with my driver's license.

Which is really, really small.

And also, not a great picture of me.

I wake up as we pull into a gas station. "Where are we?" I ask, rubbing my eyes. I hear the back car door slam and see Zena running into the convenience store.

"Get her!" my mother almost screams, and several other people pumping gas look around to see who the lunatic is.

"Mom, it's *okay*," I insist as I climb out of the car. As soon as everyone stops looking at us, I rearrange my shirt and shorts, which luckily I am wearing, unlike in my dream, and run off to follow my sister. I do a lot of this, or I used to. She's a bolter.

I find her browsing by the candy. Not that I can fault her for this. "You can't do that," I say.

"Do what? Buy M&M's?" she asks. "Why, because they're not Skittles?"

"Ha-ha. No, I meant, take off, run into places by yourself," I say. "You're, you know. Vulnerable." I look around the store, where various people of various ages are buying various road foods. There's a giant case of knives over by the trucking supplies area that makes me wonder.

"I am not," Zena insists.

"Please. You're twelve. The 'v' in twelve is for vulnerable," I say. "You're twelvulnerable."

"Am not," she argues.

"Do you ever watch the news? Girls like you disappear every day." I look around for Skittles and see an empty display box, which just figures. This trip is off on the wrong foot in every way.

Zena edges a little closer to me. "I know what I'm doing."

"Fine."

"Mom is driving like a bat out of hell," Zena comments after we visit the restroom and buy some bottled water. "Why?"

"Um, because that's how she is? Because she's trying to be like Dad?" I suggest.

We sip our water and browse the postcard rack. Apparently we left Wisconsin while I was sleeping, and now we're in Minnesota. I'm flipping through postcards on the metal spinning racks and get bored and think if I spin the rack faster and faster we will go past those places faster and faster.

Suddenly the rack stops spinning and I hear this "Ow. Geez." And some other words I won't bother repeating.

There's a man standing on the other side of the postcard rack. He's tall, oldish, and has a strange mustache with twirly yet droopy ends, as if it can't make up its mind whether to stay on his face or not.

"Quit it," he says, glowering at me.

"You quit it," I say back.

We start wrestling with the postcard rack, which I can't believe I'm doing, except I was here first and I did have my eye on a goofy loon postcard and I don't think just anyone should be able to turn the rack when I'm already looking at it.

He sees Zena and all of a sudden he gets this gleam in his eyes. He smiles at her and says, "What's *your* name?"

She doesn't answer and I start to tell him it's none of his business, but he repeats, "What's your name? I want to buy you an ice cream." And he smiles his creepy smile with his creepy mouth and his droopy mustache and it's like I see his reflection in the knife case and suddenly know why it exists.

"Let's get out of here," I tell Zena. We run to the counter, I set down two quarters for the postcard, and we dash outside to meet Mom's waiting arms, or at least the open doors of the car. We're both laughing, and Mom wants to know why, because it's probably strange to see us having fun together.

"What happened?" she asks.

"Oh, nothing," Zena says.

Mom taps the top of the car. "Let's go, girls. We have a schedule to keep."

"We do? I thought we had a realoose itinerary," I say.

"Well, we do. But because of our motel reservation, we've got to get to Sioux Falls by five," Mom says.

"Sioux Falls. South Dakota. Why?" I ask.

She smiles as we all get into the car. "You'll see."

I hadn't really been paying attention until now, but I notice the road signs. We're heading west. Just like Dylan. "What do you mean, Mom? Where are we going?"

"To the starting point for our journey," she says.

"But we already started. In Milwaukee," Zena points out as she buckles her seat belt.

"Where we begin is not necessarily our starting point. Every journey has its mileposts," Mom says.

I roll my eyes at her psychobabble, then stare out the window at a mile marker as we get onto the highway again, and wonder what it is supposed to mean.

Dad used to take us on cross-country tours like this, but it was always rushed. We'd have to see this place and that place, and we'd do it all in one week.

We should have been suspicious last summer when we drove out east to Atlantic City, but we weren't. We enjoyed the ocean and the visit into New York City and we never once considered the reason he was so exhausted was because he didn't sleep at night; he sneaked out to the casinos. Which is why I'll be attending community college unless I can win a track scholarship.

"After South Dakota, then what?" Zena asks, leaning over the front seat.

"I have some surprises up my sleeve." Mom's sleeves being organic cotton and baggy, they're bound to fall out soon. But it reminds me of something Dad always said about cards up his sleeve, and it must remind Mom too, because her nose wrinkles as if she's just tasted the bottom of a bag of dill-pickle chips and gotten a mouthful of extra-sour pickle-chip powder.

The loon is the Minnesota state bird. Listen for its plaintive call.

Sarah,
Beware of strange men in truck stops offering free ice cream.
   That's all I'm saying.
   Also, my mom is crazy. But we knew that.
   Miss you and wish you were here instead.
   Zena has already run off once and doesn't believe she is a target.
      Yours until I get abducted (not that it would happen because I'll outrun them),
      AF

I...ll...ll..l.lll...ll....ll...ll..l.l.l.lll.l.l.l..l.ll

Chapter Four

For dinner we head to a diner across the street from the motel where we've checked in for the night in Sioux Falls.

Mom seems very excited about dinner, which is odd, since we're headed to a place called Matt's Turkey Diner. Clearly she's feeling the romance, the intrigue of being on the road. She hasn't seemed "up" like this very much lately, and now she's getting excited about turkey.

"Turkey dinner," Zena says out loud. "Yum."

"No, turkey diner," I correct.

"Who ever heard of a turkey diner?" Zena says.

Mom loops her arm through Zena's as we cross the street. "Isn't that what we're about to be, if we eat turkey?"

"You guys maybe," I say. "I'm not dining on any turkey."

"But it's the specialty," Mom insists. "The motel manager said it was the best food around."

"If they told you wolverines would make good house pets, would you believe them?" I say, quoting my favorite line from the movie *Planes, Trains and Automobiles*.

My mother's gullibility has been duly noted and recorded in county court transcripts. You'd think she'd become a little more suspicious with age.

Inside, the place reminds me of Luke's diner on *Gilmore Girls*, but without the witty banter and the cuteness.

I order blueberry pancakes. "Hold the turkey," I say. The waitress looks at me with narrowed eyes, as if the fact she has to serve breakfast all day is *my* fault.

Mom orders a piece of apple pie à la mode to start, which is her famous restaurant move, ordering dessert first and occasionally last as well, and then she has a turkey sandwich with potatoes, and a café mocha with whipped cream. The woman can put food away.

Zena puts ketchup on her open-face roast turkey sandwich. She covers everything with ketchup, as if she's still six. She has a milk shake (ketchup-free), while I sip iced tea and take a bite of my pancakes. The door opens and in walks this incredibly hot guy, Brad Pitt in his *Thelma and Louise/Seven* early years, pre-Brangelina. He looks like he's maybe eighteen or so. He has a very tan face and spiky blond hair and he looks like he's already been working outside all summer, though it's only June. Not only does he have muscles, they're tan muscles.

He gives me this long look before he sits down at the counter. Maple syrup drips down my arm because I've been holding my bite in midair for too long.

It's the sexiest moment of my life.

So far.

But I shouldn't be noticing him, even if he is staring at me. I shouldn't be looking at any other guys. Counter Boy looks nice, sure.

But he's probably not half as nice or interesting as Dylan.

But then I remember Dylan's phone call and him saying, "What happens on the road, stays on the road." And this is as "on the road" as it gets.

Just as I'm about to get up and go talk to Counter Boy, trying to think of some pretext, Zena announces that she needs more ketchup and walks up to the counter, right beside him.

She is such a horrible flirt and she's only twelve. It is really embarrassing—or impressive, depending on how you look at it. She has the body I'm supposed to have at sixteen, and vice versa.

Naturally, I drop my fork and jump up to follow her. It's my job to rein her in, according to my mother. When I get to the counter, Zena is laughing and telling the guy that yes, turkey and ketchup do go together. "Tastes great," she says.

"Less filling?" he replies with a sexy smile.

I wait for an opening, shuffling closer. "Excuse my crazy sister," I say, but as I reach for the ketchup in Zena's hand, I slip, and my syrup-covered hand ends up grabbing Brad Pitt Jr.'s arm. I try to pull it away, and there's a sucking sound, and I think some of his arm hair is coming off. "Sorry," I say, thinking it's very embarrassing to be literally stuck to someone.

"It's okay," he says as he dips a napkin in his water glass and brushes his arm with it. "You guys are *really* into ketchup, huh?" he asks. When he smiles at me, I notice he has these crystal-clean white teeth and is even cuter up close. I don't know how to make a move, but I know I should be making one. I could just kiss him right now and it would be totally random and exciting.

Before I can make a move of any kind, though, there's someone tapping on my shoulder. I turn, expecting my mom. But it's not her; it's a man.

It takes a second to register who this person is. No, he's not some random forty-year-old being too friendly, in an invading-myspace.com kind of way.

It's my uncle Jeff.

In the flesh. Lots and lots of flesh.

"Uncle Jeff? What are you . . ." I start to say as he smiles at me. As Counter Boy gets set to eat his turkey burger, Zena screams, "Hey!" and hugs Uncle Jeff.

"You guys look fantasterrific," Uncle Jeff says as he smushes me in a group hug with Zena. It's like being hugged by a friendly grizzly, not that those exist.

Mom rushes over and slips her arm through Uncle Jeff's as he stands back to give us a breath. "Zena, Ariel? I have a surprise for you. We're not driving across the country," she says with a big grin.

"We're not? Yes!" Zena high-fives me, with my syrupy, sticky hand that was once destined for and connected to Counter Boy.

"Are we having a family reunion?" I ask. "In Sioux Falls?" Is there something about our family history I don't know, some unclaimed clan of cousins nearby?

"In a manner of speaking, it's a reunion, yes. We're not driving across the country, because we're traveling by bus," Mom says. "It's a ten-day tour, with Uncle Jeff and Grandma and Grandpa Timmons!"

I cough. My throat is suddenly closing up. Either I'm allergic to Matt's Turkey Diner's maple syrup, or I'm allergic to bus trips. Either way, I can't breathe. "What?" I gasp.

Grandma and Grandpa Timmons are already on their way over to us, big smiles on their faces.

I always used to call them "Tims-moms" when I was little, because I couldn't pronounce it right. "Cinnamon," Grandma T.

would say, over and over. "It's just like cinnamon." Which, honestly, I still don't get.

My grandmother kisses my cheek, and her silver-blond hair smells like permanent dye the way it always does, which makes my eyes water. It's cut short and sleek, and goes with her *velour du jour*, as I call them. She's famous for wearing the latest in trendy track-suits, hoodies, and loungewear. She's about a size four, tiny.

My grandfather, never a big hugger, stands back a little and claps me on the back, but seems as genuinely happy as anyone to be here. He retired recently, and although he isn't wearing a starched busi-ness suit right now, he still seems like he is.

I haven't seen them since Easter, when they came to help us move into our new, smaller house. It's definitely a shock.

"Can you believe this? Isn't this going to be fantasterrific?" Uncle Jeff, whom I call "Lord of the Necklaces," asks. He insists on wear-ing this gold cross, plus a necklace with a gold boat propeller charm, and a necklace with a little gold envelope.

He was a mailman until he was attacked by a family of squirrels, who dropped out of a tree onto his head, probably because he was talking too long to the house's resident and had bored the squirrels to death.

We had to drive up to St. Paul to visit him in the hospital where he was getting rabies shots. It was very traumatic, the whole squirrel attack and its aftermath, so now he's on disability, which is when he gained fifty pounds, which *is* kind of a disability.

Uncle Jeff hands me a box of Dots. "You still love these, right?"

"No," I say, "but thanks."

He looks a bit wounded. "I thought you loved chewy fruit candies and things of that nature."

"Skittles," I say. "Those are the ones."

"Oh. Well." He shrugs. "If I were you, I'd keep them anyway. We've got lots of travel days coming up. Need some road food." He smiles and sort of half punches my shoulder.

"Yes. We do." I smile at him. "We sure . . . do.

"Mother. What were you thinking?" I ask in a harsh whisper as we reshuffle our seats and make room, finally sitting down in a larger booth.

"You need a positive male influence in your lives," she says.

"Why do we need a male influence? We have Dad," I argue.

"I said *positive*."

I suppose Uncle Jeff is positive. In a very revolting, sickeningly sweet kind of way.

"That's why we could only let you bring the bare minimum luggage," my mother explains. "Because the bus has certain specifications; there are size restrictions for everyone's bags."

"You know, this sounds kind of exciting, if you ask me." Zena shrugs.

"We didn't." I glare at her. What would she know about exciting? "Where are we going?"

"We're going to see the Heartland," Uncle Jeff says proudly, as if he devised the tour. If he did, we're in more trouble than I thought. The man believes that birch trees are interesting. Birch. Trees.

"The Heartland," I repeat. What exactly does that mean, anyway? As if one part of the country is better than another, is more central and more vital to keeping it going. Where is the Liverland? The Kidneyland?

"We start here in South Dakota, and spend several days exploring it," Mom says. "Then we're off to—"

"North Dakota?" I suggest.

"Well, I don't know—that's one of the hallmarks of this tour company. They keep a few things a surprise."

"Up their sleeves," I mutter.

"What's the point of surprising us? You'd think they'd want us to know where we're going," my grandfather says.

"Exactly," I chime in.

"Don't be so rigid. This is going to be a totally new way to experience things," Mom says. "We can look around more and enjoy the scenery."

And I can enjoy the scenery of being trapped with fifty strangers, I think. "But, um, Mom?" I say, trying to be civil, trying not to scream about this.

"Yes, honey?"

"How am I going to keep up with my running?" I ask.

"Oh, we'll have plenty of pit stops. Same as if we were driving. Whenever we stop for a tour, or a hotel—you know, you can fit it in." She smiles.

I want to throttle her. She doesn't understand that I plan on winning the state cross-country championship this year. She has completely forgotten all about how I was third last year and how I want to move up. She acts as if this is an afterthought.

"I'll run with you, Ariel," my grandfather offers, and it's sweet, but ridiculous, because he's sixty-five, so I just pat his shoulder and smile like a good granddaughter.

"Can't we all just rent an RV or something?" I ask.

"Oh no," says Uncle Jeff. "This will be much, much better. We'll have a tour guide. We'll meet new people. It'll be great!" He stands up to snap our picture with a camera that looks decidedly undigital.

I slide out of the booth and go back over to the counter, where the cute guy is now eating an ice-cream sundae. "You're not by any chance going on a bus tour tomorrow, are you?" I ask.

"A what?" he says.

"A bus tour?" I repeat.

He shakes his head.

"Yeah. I didn't think so." I look back at our oversize booth, at my oversize mom and uncle.

Suddenly I notice the diner is full of retired-looking people, turkey diners here for the last meal before they hit the road.

The last supper.

Our final meal before execution.

And I want to sob.

I turn back to the guy. "You don't by any chance *drive* a bus?"

The Rainbow Lanes and Motor Lodge
Where every morning is a good morning! Sleep on our deluxe
full-size mattresses. Enjoy in-room shower and iron.

Hey Dylan—
We are at a really awful motel in South
Dakota tonight. Wish you were here.

And then I look at the postcard and realize I have to rip it up, because you can't tell a guy you want him to be in a motel room with you.

Not even if you sort of do.

The postcard is so old and outdated that after one rip, it crumbles onto the floor.

Matt's Turkey Diner: because you should never be too far from a hot turkey sandwich and some real mashed potatoes. Twenty-five years of talking turkey. Eat in or take out. Buses welcome.

Dylan,
You won't believe this. We're busing it.
    My uncle Jeff and grandparents are here, too.
    It's a Family Re-Union. On Wheels. The wheels on the bus go round and round. Etc.
    I regret that I have but one bus ride to give for my country.
    And this will be it.
    Your favorite patriot,
    Ariel
    P.S. Wish you were here, or I was there.

Chapter Five

The next morning we meet at the world headquarters of Leisure-Lee Tours, which is a sentence I never thought I'd write.

It's not exactly world headquarters; it's a small white stucco building with two buses parked out front—one old and one new.

There's a parking lot for everyone to leave their cars, and as we walk away from ours, I cast a longing glance over my shoulder at the old Jetta. What once seemed so horrible, those long family car trips, now seems like the Good Old Days. No, the Great Old Days.

The two buses bear the image of a guy wearing a leisure suit and lying sideways, and the name "Leisure-Lee" is written in script with big loopy Ls that kind of trail off like exhaust. "See the U.S. at *your* pace!" it says underneath him.

My pace? That would be really, really quickly. Let's pause in each state, see the highlights, then move on and get home. I like the sound of this. But I don't think that's what they mean. I think they mean that this is a bus for people who don't want to move all that quickly from place to place.

There are mostly senior citizens, but it isn't all older people. Just ninety-nine percent. There are one or two other families like us. There's a girl who looks like she could be Zena's age, and not-quite-identical-but-very-close twin boys who look like they're maybe in high school. They have short, bright blond hair and identical gold-frame glasses and Adidas soccer shirts.

I walk over to them to introduce myself, but then I hear them talking to their parents and realize they may be the only people my age on the bus, but English is not their first language. Poor, pitiful souls like me being dragged by their parents who are attempting to save gas money. In another country.

"Hi," I say, feeling really stupid and American.

"Hello," they say in unison, while their parents vigorously shake Mom's hand and say they are from Germany and can't wait to see more of our country.

Meanwhile, Zena and the other girl are chatting like they're long-lost sisters, instead of us.

That's it. The rest of the passengers are older people. Significantly older. I'm dying. Or I will die of boredom on this trip. And when I do, I'll probably have company.

We're standing there semi-cluelessly, wondering where to go next, when the newer bus's door opens, and two insanely cheerful people step down onto the pavement in front of us.

"Welcome, welcome, tourists!" the man says. He has pants and a shirt with many pockets, an Australian accent, and a hat with flaps. "My name's Lenny; I'm here to entertain you, tell you folks about the stops, keep things moving—"

"And I'm Jenny," the woman next to him says, no accent, but similar getup, as if she shops at REI and she's going hiking soon. "I'll be keeping things moving because I'll be driving the bus! Hello, hello, everyone!" She raises her hands over her head as if she's just won a heavyweight bout, as if she's Million-Dollar Baby. "We were just doing a final safety inspection of the bus; you'll be glad to know it passed with flying colors."

"We've vacuumed every seat. We've dusted every armrest. If this is not the cleanest bus in America, you can call me a koala," Lenny says.

My grandfather frowns. "Koala?" he says.

"I thought that was New Zealand," my grandmother comments.

"Australia has the best stamps. Don't you think?" my uncle asks. "Especially the Sydney Olympics special edition. Those were keepers. I might have one on here." He takes off his floppy khaki hat, which is covered with pins he had made out of laminated stamps, and turns it around, searching.

Lenny and Jenny walk around to meet us personally. Jenny can't quite get over Zena's name, she loves it so much. "*Xena: Warrior Princess* was my favorite show!"

We have no idea who or what she's talking about, but we nod and smile and make nice, because this is what we've been trained to do, like circus seals.

"Well, how's everyone doing over here?" Lenny asks. He makes the rounds, introducing himself, and I can't help noticing his handshake is sort of an insincere clasp, a little on the dead-fish side.

"Pleased to meet you, Lenny. I have a question. Did you know Steve Irwin?" my uncle asks, referring to the famed crocodile hunter.

Lenny looks at Uncle Jeff as if he can't quite believe his ears. "No. I did not have the good fortune. Australia is a very large country, you know."

"I just thought, you're both in the media-slash-entertainment profession," Uncle Jeff says. "Maybe you'd met."

Lenny shakes his head. "No."

"Huh. Well, it's a small world sometimes, but then sometimes it's a big world. Take my postal route, for example." He starts telling people how much he loves delivering mail because it, and I quote, "brings sunshine to lonely people." He has this knack for engaging everyone in conversation. Whether they want him to or not. He likes to know his neighbors and his postees, as he calls them. "There's nothing like the feeling of delivering a birthday card. You just know you're making someone's day."

"You always say that, but what if it's a condolence card?" Grandpa Timmons asks. "A sympathy card? How can you tell what it is?"

"After a while you just know. It's the way people's handwriting looks. And, of course, glitter," Uncle Jeff says. "Sometimes it falls out."

"People put glitter in sympathy cards?" someone else wonders out loud, not quite getting it.

Jenny hands us luggage tags and "Hello My Name Is" tags. I fill out the first, but leave the name tag blank. I can't—and don't—see anyone else wearing the name badges, not even the older folks. Besides, do I really want to hear forty-five people ask me if I was named after the Little Mermaid?

A car pulls up in the little circular drive in front of the building, and an African American woman gets out of one side, while a tall guy who looks like her teenage son, maybe, gets out of the other. They're the last people to show up, so we all can't help noticing them, because we've been hanging around for a while, listening to the Lenny and Jenny Show.

The guy opens the trunk of the car and starts hauling out suitcases. He has light brown skin and cool rectangular glasses that make him look intellectual. He looks like he's my age, or maybe a little older. He's wearing a T-shirt with the message, WHOSE AUTHORITY?, long shorts, and low-cut sneakers with no socks.

He looks cool. I can't believe it. He's here to save me, to save this trip from being the death of me.

Then I think: Maybe he's not actually getting on the bus; maybe he's just dropping off his *mom*. That would not be cool. That would be one of the universe's many cruel jokes.

His mom stands there and supervises, lifting only a small bag out herself. She and my mom could wear the same size, somewhere around XL, except this woman is too well dressed to trade clothes with my mom. Let me put it this way: She has Outfits. Mom has Stay-In-fits.

"Excuse me, Jeffrey," Lenny says to my uncle as he walks past us and heads for the newly arrived passengers. "Hello, there! You must be the O'Neills. A pleasure to meet you. I'm Lenny."

My ears perk up. He said O'Neills. Plural.

"Hi, Lenny. Yes, I'm Lorraine, and this is my son, Andre."

"That's terrific. We're so glad you're here." Lenny clasps his hands together. "Now for the bad news. I'm sorry, but you'll have to scuttle a few of those bags."

"Scuttle?" she repeats.

"Compact. Compress. Discard," her son says.

"Oh no." She shakes her head. "I couldn't."

"I'm sorry, madam, but you'll have to. This trip is all about personal growth, except in this case, where it's about personal reduction."

"What are you implying?" she says, hands on her hips.

"Your luggage. That's all I meant." Lenny holds up four fingers, like he's used to dealing with people who don't speak English and has to use body language to communicate. "Because some people underpacked, I can give you room for four bags, maximum."

"That's not fair," someone else chimes in. "It was one per person."

"One large per person," someone else says.

"Not one per large person?" someone else adds, and everyone laughs.

This is bus humor. Or elder humor. Apparently.

"No, it's one large suitcase per traveler, one small," Jenny explains, again with the counting-on-fingers method.

"Define small," Mrs. O'Neill says, her eyes narrowed at Jenny.

"Forty-five linear inches." Lenny pulls a measuring tape out of his khaki pants pocket, which seems to carry a plethora of assorted supplies. They're the kind of pants with multiple pockets and zippers. So far I've seen him extract a Swiss Army knife, a screwdriver, a ball of twine, and a flashlight. "Let's have a look," he says, and starts to measure the suitcases.

"Well, this is just plain ridiculous," Mrs. O'Neill complains. "Are we supposed to dress like slobs just because we're on a bus?"

"Ma, I told you about the luggage limit, okay? So don't act surprised. Here, I'll get rid of one of my bags," her son offers. Then he smiles. "No, wait—I know. I won't go! Then you can use my seat for all *your* luggage."

I smile, biting my lip.

"Very funny, Andre," his mother says. "Just repack."

"Seriously, Ma. If there's not enough room—"

"Andre? Don't start with me."

"Fine." He starts randomly tearing clothes out of his large bag and jamming them into a smaller suitcase. He shows his mother an empty large suitcase. "I'll stick this back in the car, which means we can bring another bag of yours. My clothes are completely smashed and wrinkled, but as long as *you're* happy."

"I am. Thanks, sweetheart."

"Whatever," he says. After Lenny measures and approves the remaining bags, Andre carries them over to the bus, while his mom goes to park the car in the lot. I try to make eye contact, thinking I could introduce myself, let him know I feel his pain, but he's not looking at me—or at any of us.

"All right!" Lenny says once Mrs. O'Neill is back. "Everyone's here now; everyone's bagged and tagged. Wonderful. Come on now, gather 'round," he says, like we're not all standing beside the bus, waiting to get onto it. "Are you ready for the adventure of a lifetime?" Lenny asks. He waits for our response, but there isn't one. "I said, are you ready for the adventure of a lifetime?" He cocks his head to the side, holding his hand behind his ear.

"Yes!" everyone over sixty cries. Well, everyone except my grandparents.

"Great, that's great, but you're going to have to work on your cheers, all right? If you want Lee to come out here, he's going to need a big welcome. One, two, three, say it with me . . . are you ready for the adventure of a lifetime?"

"YES!" everyone screams, just as an elderly man totters out of the Leisure-Lee office. He looks frightened to death by our voices, and he walks a little unsteadily down a ramp to the parking lot. "Folks. Nice to see you," he says. He's wearing a cowboy hat and aviator sunglasses. I glance at the illustration on the bus, and then at him. Yes, it's the same guy.

"So you're retired now?" Uncle Jeff asks him.

"Oh no. Never retire!" Leisure-Lee says, waving his cane in the air. "Once you retire, you don't get vacation."

"Hm. An interesting perspective," Uncle Jeff comments.

Leisure-Lee starts to wobble a little, and Jenny quickly fetches a chair from inside the office. He sits down. The years on the road have clearly taken a toll.

"Now, our name Leisure-Lee Tours says it all. Most tour bus companies rush you from place to place." Lenny shakes his head. "Not us. Never have done, never will."

"Oh, great." I sigh.

"Shh," Zena says.

"You want to see something? We see it. We don't believe in rushing you through your vacation. Why? Because when life gives you a vacation, what do you do?" He waits for a second. "You take it! By the horns.

"Now, we'll see all the notable sites, but without the hustle, without the bustle. We want you to enjoy your vacation. Put your feet up. Relax. Have a little time for some introspection. In fact, we're the only bus tour out there committed to your personal growth."

My mother looks over at me and smiles, like a bit of a know-it-all. Of course, personal growth is one of her buzzwords, like "realsimple," and it's also "realconnected" to Mom's line of work, so of course she found a bus company that espouses it.

In reality, though, my mother the counselor, the expert on women's personal health and growth issues, was living with an addictive personality. For years. That chapter in her book called *Talk It Out, Work It Out* about healthy relationships? Pure fiction.

"Our founder, Lee, believes that life is all about seeing the small stuff," Lenny says.

Leisure-Lee nods. "Damn right."

Life is also all about eating the small stuff. I take out a handful of Skittles. If it would be possible for a meteor to hurtle from the sky right now and hit the bus as we head out on the open road? I'd be all for that. As long as it took out the bus, but missed the people. And our car.

Jenny then makes us introduce ourselves, and it starts to feel like a new season of *The Amazing Race*, and everyone will have little captions floating under them like:

GARY & BETTY, MARRIED

KRISTY & ROGER, RETIRED

LENNY & JENNY, MARRIED BUS HOSTS

and

THE FLACK FAMILY, SLIGHTLY INSANE

or

THE FLACKS, NO OUR DAD ISN'T HERE, DOING JUST FINE, THANKS

There may not be enough Skittles in South Dakota to get me through this trip.

"Find your own friend, A," Zena says when I get on the bus ten minutes later, expecting to sit with her.

Like I said, my little sister is not exactly supportive. "Z, there's nowhere else to sit," I say out of the corner of my mouth, feeling like I've landed in junior high all of a sudden and I should be holding a lunch tray. Mom is sitting with Uncle Jeff, while Grandma and Grandpa are sitting together. It's all in the family. Except for me.

"Right here, young lady!" Lenny points to a seat toward the front. "Right this way."

I pick up my backpack of Minimum Daily Requirements—pens, postcards, Skittles, lip balm, and a book—and head to the front of the bus. I see Mrs. O'Neill sitting with a gray-haired woman with a name tag that says "ETHEL" in giant letters, and across the aisle from them is an empty seat next to her son.

He glances up at Lenny and then over at me. "I have to sit up front. I get carsick," he explains. "Bus-sick, I mean."

"Great," I say, perching on the edge of the empty seat.

"Not *sick* sick, just kind of woozy. Hey, you want the window?" he offers.

"Sure," I say.

"That way if I do hurl, it'll be into the aisle," he says.

I wish he hadn't given me that image to worry about. "Thanks."

"Joking. Joshing. Not serious. Hey, have you heard the new Beck?" he asks, bobbing his head slightly and pulling out an iPod. He has a vintage baseball cap on, and the brim is starting to slide down over his face. "It's fantastic. Amazing. Incredible," he adds, I guess in case I don't know what "fantastic" means. He flips down the tray on the seat back, the kind they have on airplanes. He gets out this vocabulary book and a highlighter and starts reading, or skimming, or memorizing.

Highlighters make a very annoying sound if you're not the one wearing an iPod. Which I'm not. So it pretty much sucks. I stare out the window and wish I knew more about where we were going, so I could start counting down the mile markers, or counting them up, or something.

I excuse myself and go two rows up to Lenny, who's sitting in the seat right behind Jenny, who's driving. "Excuse me. Is there a bus postcard?" I ask Lenny.

"Please?" he replies.

I can't believe he's going to insist on manners. "Is there a bus postcard, please?" I ask.

"No, mate, I didn't hear you, that's all," Lenny says with a chuckle. "You want a postcard?"

I nod. "Something that's, you know, promotional or something. About the bus."

"No problem." Lenny reaches into a small compartment behind

the driver's seat and rummages around. Finally he pulls out a faded, dated postcard that looks as if it were made when color cameras were still new, when bus tours were still cool. It shows Lee, about fifty years ago, sitting in the driver's seat, beckoning people aboard a silver bus.

"I've only got the one," Lenny says as he hands it to me.

"One is perfect," I say. I go back to my seat and slide past iPod vocab guy. He gives me a questioning look and I hold up the postcard, as if to justify myself and my journey down the aisle and back.

In case he's wondering if I went up to ask for something embarrassing like a tampon. Not that I'd ask Lenny. Of course I'd ask Jenny.

I get out a pen and start to write. Already I have a lot to write home about.

"So." My neighbor takes off his headphones. "I'm Andre."

"Hi. I'm Ariel," I say.

"Like the mermaid."

I smile, but not happily.

"So, how did you get onto the bus?" he asks.

"Steps?" I suggest.

He laughs. "Really. Because I was dragged. Kicking and screaming."

"I didn't notice that," I say.

"You were probably too busy kicking and screaming yourself. Couldn't hear me."

"Exactly. What, you mean you're not thrilled to be spending ten days on a bus?" I ask him in a soft voice.

"I'm giving this trip two days, max," he says. "Then I'm ditching."

Just as he says that, music starts to blare out of the bus speakers. It's the soundtrack to the musical *Oklahoma!*

"Hey, you want to listen to this instead?" he asks, nudging my shoulder and pointing to his iPod.

I shrug. "No, it's okay," I say, wondering if he really means that part about ditching the bus. I hadn't thought seriously of that yet, except in my overactive fantasy life, as I lay awake the night before listening to my mother snore.

"Really. It's cool. You can have half." He takes out one earbud and hands it to me.

"My mom made me leave my MP3 at home because she wanted us to *talk*," I explain as we shift positions and get comfortable. "Not that it's very good anyway; it was a bribe from my dad. Only he didn't buy a good one, so it wasn't much of a bribe."

"Parents." He smiles a little sadly. "Here." And we listen together. After Beck, some of the music I don't know but some of it I do, and it's nice even if it's only one ear's worth.

After a few minutes, when we're on the highway, he points out the window and I follow his gaze and see a gas station with a red flashing sign that alternates between:

EAT

GAS

EAT

GAS

EAT

GAS

I look at him.

"No comment," he says, and we both smile. It's the first time I've smiled hearing those two words together in a long time.

Dylan!

You won't believe this.

I'm trapped on a tour bus with my relatives.

And other crazy people.

And two overly chipper tour guides.

It's some crazy plan to get us to bond while seeing the USA.

Wish u were here instead.

Ariel

l,,,ll,,,ll,,ll,,l,lll,,,,ll,,,,ll,,,ll,,l,l,,l,ll,l,,l,,l,,,,l,ll

Chapter Six

We pull off the highway and stop at a rest area for lunch. Jenny slides out a giant tray of brown-bag lunches from a chilled compartment next to our luggage. Maybe that shouldn't gross me out, but it does.

We're spread out at various tables, eating bag lunches. Or at least some people are eating them. I had so many Skittles that I really can't think about eating much else, and besides, it doesn't look all that yummy. Something about our lunch being so close to the hot pavement that we were driving over is just wrong.

"Is every lunch going to be on the road?" I ask Jenny as she smiles and sets a brown bag in front of me. I'll go through it and pull out the stuff I want to eat later, just like I do for away track and cross-country meets. The apple and the cookie can be preserved. I'll drink the soda now. The sandwich can be tossed.

"Some will be, but others we'll eat out," Jenny says. "Any place with a sign up that says, 'Buses Welcome,' we're there." She winks at me.

I study her face, feeling like I can't trust her. They're keeping secrets for some reason. I'm sure of it. They're delivering us to some strange location, like that underground storage place in Nevada. We'll all be part of some bizarre genetic study involving nuclear waste, which might be less risky than eating this lunch. It looks slightly genetically modified, as if it were built to withstand two weeks on the road, though I don't know if this is possible with cold cuts. Or would they be warm cuts?

I turn the sandwich over in my hand. It has a sticker that says, HAM 'N' CHEEZ.

Just as I'm about to throw it out, I look up at my grandfather, who's watching me.

"Um, you want this?" I ask.

He just widens his eyes. "Hell, no," he says. "I have my health to think of." And he pulls out a PowerBar for lunch.

I'm sitting at a table with my family, but I cannot make eye contact with my mother. I refuse to. She's keeping secrets these days, too. Hoarding information. She's become a hoarder. One of those weird people with fifty-seven cats, only instead of cats, it's stuff I don't know but wish that I did.

"This is so much better than driving," she keeps saying.

"How is this better than driving? And why are we here? I don't mean to sound so existential, but really, what are we doing here?" I ask before I sip my soda.

"Would anyone be willing to trade?" Uncle Jeff is asking around. "I've got a nice ham sandwich here. I'm looking for turkey."

"Here," Andre says, offering up his Turkey 'n' Tomato.

"You sure now?" Uncle Jeff asks as he reaches for the sandwich trade, like this is elementary school and he's the big, yet polite, bully.

"I'm sure," he says.

"Fantasterrific!" my uncle says.

Andre looks at me and raises one eyebrow as he hands the sandwich to Uncle Jeff. As the sandwich travels past Andre's mom, a tiny dog's head pokes up over the top of her big purse and tries to eat the turkey sandwich right out of his hand.

Uncle Jeff, with his fear of small animals due to the Great Squirrel Incident, immediately drops his ham sandwich to the ground and leaps backward. "What the—"

"Cuddles. Cuddles! He's not usually so aggressive," Mrs. O'Neill explains, as if having a dog in her purse—on a bus trip—is perfectly normal. She tries to pull back the dog, who is barking and wrestling with the sandwich, trying to eat the whole thing even though his head is tiny and his mouth is smaller than a snake's.

"Ma!" Her son looks at her with disgust. "What were you thinking? How could you even think this would work, and you lied to me, and—"

"Anyone else have turkey?" Uncle Jeff is asking as everyone gathers around to see the dog. "Turkey, anyone?"

"I'll take a turkey," one of the older passengers says, clearly having misunderstood.

"Ma. I *told* you this would happen," Andre says.

"And I told you, I couldn't leave him at home in a kennel," she says. "He's just a baby." She makes embarrassing kissy noises, saying, "Who's my favorite boy?" as she snuggles the dog to her, kissing him on the mouth but getting mostly bread.

I try to picture smuggling Gloves onto the bus. She'd yowl so loudly that we wouldn't make it up the first step.

Lenny and Jenny march over, as if they're the police, which I guess they are in this case. "All right, people. Let's talk," Lenny says.

"We don't need to *talk* about it," Jenny says. "We've got a policy to deal with situations like this. It's called no pets!"

"But perhaps there's a reason for this. A medical emergency or something," my grandmother suggests.

"What kind of medical emergency can be helped by a Chihuahua?" my mother says. "And *is* that a Chihuahua, or a rat?"

"It's nothing more than a desire to look like one of those celebrities who carry little dogs in bags," my grandfather mutters to me. "Annoying. Cruel."

"Yet occasionally stylish, depending on the dog's outfit," I add.

Lenny climbs up on a picnic table and claps his hands to get everyone's attention, as if everyone's not already gathered around staring at the dog. "All right, everyone. Listen up. Now, the first thing we need to investigate is whether anyone in this group is allergic to dogs?"

He waits a second, but nobody claims to be.

"He's a very well-behaved dog," Andre's mom speaks up. "He's completely potty-trained, and you haven't heard him bark once, have you? He sleeps like an angel cuddled next to me. That's why I named him Cuddles."

Andre looks at me and rolls his eyes. I realize that maybe the two of us are going to get along, because I start thinking how much both our moms are annoying us right now. It isn't much to bond over, but it's something.

"I'll pay an extra fee, if need be," Mrs. O'Neill offers. "A pet deposit. Whatever you want. But please, please, don't ask me to leave him behind."

Andre adds, "Plus, she'll go insane if she has to leave the dog somewhere, and then we'll have an insane woman on the bus."

I glance at my mother. Two insane women on the bus.

"Nobody wants anybody to lose her mind on this trip, I can assure you," Lenny says. "That happened to us on a tour once. Middle of

Arizona. Woman went stark raving mad in the desert. Had to get her flown out by helicopter."

"That sounds promising. Do you think Mom did *any* research on this bus company?" I ask my grandfather.

He smiles at me. "Yes, she did, because she called us about a dozen times to ask if we thought this was a good idea."

"And you said . . . ?" I ask.

"Hey, we'll do anything to spend time with you guys," he replies with a shrug. "Well. Almost anything. We put the kibosh on a nature retreat with a bunch of life-coach seminars."

"Thank you." I sigh, turning my attention back to the dog debate.

"The issue is whether we let both of you stay on the bus," Jenny says. "This is a major infraction of the rules."

Mrs. O'Neill looks at her with narrowed eyes. "If I go, then my son goes," she says. "We'll demand a full refund. And that's two paid passengers you won't be able to replace at the last minute."

"Perhaps a surcharge, then," Lenny says nervously, "would be the best solution."

"No, we have to go by our published policy for situations like this," Jenny states with a meaningful glare at her hubby. "We're bringing it to a bus vote. Bus votes are what we do when we have conflicts. So. How many people are in favor of letting Cuddles stay on the bus?"

As I stand there watching some of the older passengers' hands shake as they hold them in the air, I realize that if the dog goes, Andre goes, and he is the only person on the bus I could remotely bond with, and he let me listen to his iPod.

I raise my hand as high as I can. "Let them stay on the bus," I say. "I bet half of us have pets at home that we miss." I look around the crowd and see everyone watching me. Why am I doing this, again?

"And unlike my cat, Gloves? Cuddles is transportable. He doesn't whine, or scratch, or demand to be let on and off the bus." Unlike me, too, I think. "So maybe Cuddles could be, like . . . our mascot. Every bus—every team—needs a mascot. Right? Like at my school, we're the mighty Panthers, and so it cheers us all up when the Panther's on the bus—"

"You have a live panther?"

"Oh, jeez, that'd worry me."

"Anyway," I say. "What's the harm in letting Cuddles stay? Maybe he could be like our, uh, therapy dog."

"Ooh!" my mother cries. "Great idea."

"But he's going to make it impossible for us to gain entrance to certain sites," someone complains.

"You'd be surprised. The policies on pets are changing everywhere," Mrs. O'Neill says. "He does have lots of cute outfits. He'll charm his way in."

"We can't hang out here any longer talking about this. Who's for Cuddles?" Jenny asks again. "Raise your hands."

Lenny counts the votes. "Thirty-three. That carries. The bus has spoken. Cuddles the Chihuahua . . . welcome to Leisure-Lee Country, where the miles and smiles aren't far apart." He reaches over to rub the dog's head, but Cuddles looks like he'd rather chew his hand.

As we meander back over to the bus, Andre comes up to me. "I don't know whether to kiss you or to kill you."

I feel my face turn red. "What?"

"That dog was my chance. To escape. And you blew it for me," he says as we stand in line to get back onto the bus.

"Sorry," I say. "I didn't think—"

He shrugs. "No, it's okay. I was joking. If we had to leave, I'd go home, and that's not where I want to spend the summer either," he admits.

"I hear you," I say. "Sort of."

"So is your mom as nuts as mine?"

"Probably," I say.

"My mom picked this tour because she wants us to bond," he says. "One, I get carsick on buses, which makes it hard to read; two, she brings the dog; three, we're, like, in the middle of nowhere, and could anyone stare at us more? All these old people want to kill us."

"What? No, they don't."

"Look at them." He subtly points to a couple of retirees who are regarding us with what can only be called skepticism. Or contempt. Or hatred.

"Probably they don't like anyone under the age of twenty," I say. "One of those ageist things."

"Teen hatred. Right. I'm sure."

"So, *are* you and your mom bonding yet?" I ask.

"Like rubber cement," he says. "Epoxy. Gorilla Glue."

"Really?"

"No. More like dry Scotch tape."

"I could go for a dry Scotch," my grandfather says with a sigh as he stands behind us in line to get back on the bus.

Look for the evasive jackalope—a legendary creature feared and respected by all who visit the American West. Able to run and hop at high speeds.

Dear Gloves,
I miss you. There is a dog on the bus. It's an outrage.
But you don't like riding in cars, so I doubt you'd like buses.
Because who does, really?
Go tell Grandma you're hungry for some chopped tuna. Starving, actually.
You've never been so hungry in your life.
XX OO
A

|..,||..,||.,|.|||..,,|||,,,,||,.,||,.|,|.,|,||,|,|,|,.,,,|,||

Chapter Seven

Here's another sentence I never thought I'd write: I think the Corn Palace is cool.

In case you haven't been there, it's this giant place covered in corn kernels. I don't think I can even describe it all that well, except to say that they have a theme every summer, and there are murals made out of different-colored corn kernels. Like, when you were little and didn't want to eat your vegetables, and you made a pattern on your plate of green beans and corn.

My grandmother has taken my mother and Zena to see the Enchanted World Doll Museum across the street. I bowed out and am killing time at the Corn Palace gift shop. Naturally I'm looking at the postcards, trying to find my next victim, when I try to spin the rack and it goes nowhere. I see a blue blur on the other side that looks like Zena's hoodie, so I say, "What's your name, what's your name, I want to buy you an ice cream," in a creepy, twangy voice, the way we've been doing whenever we talk to each other, which isn't often.

But the person on the other side doesn't respond and just keeps pushing at the postcard rack, trying to spin it, and my hand gets kind of wrenched.

"Oh my god, Zena, would you *stop* it?" I say, but then I see Andre step out on the other side.

"Don't call me Zena," he says. "I have enough problems without being called a girl."

"That's my sister," I say. "And you're right."

"Where is she? Where's your mother?"

"Across the street," I say.

"Same."

So far neither of us has asked about dads, and I like that.

He looks at the collection of postcards I'm holding, which are all fairly goofy. "You need a lot of postcards," he observes.

"I'm sending them to a bunch of people. Plus I want to save some for myself," I say. "Otherwise, who will ever believe I went on this amazing trip?" I roll my eyes to let him know I'm not serious.

"Your really long and boring testimony about it should scare them off. Somewhere, there has to be a recording of that dude's presentation." He mimics Lenny and his highway narrative. "The drought was absolutely devastating to the people."

"You have a pretty good Australian accent," I say. "Where are you from?"

"Chicago," he says.

"That explains it. Isn't there a neighborhood like Little Australia? Little Sydney or something?"

"No," he says, not looking all that amused. "Anyway, I'm from outside Chicago. You?"

"Way outside Chicago. Milwaukee," I tell him. "Actually, just outside Milwaukee."

He finally laughs. "So. What will you write on your postcards about the Corn Palace?" he asks.

"That it reminds me of Russia," I say.

"You've been to Russia?"

"No, I just meant those little thingies at the top." I point to a postcard in my hand, showing him what I mean.

"The spires? Minarets," he says.

"Right. Those."

"They're mostly used in mosque construction. Islamic mosques. So I don't know what they're doing on a corn palace in South Dakota."

"Are you, um, Islamic?" I ask. Oh no, I sound like an idiot. "Muslim, I mean. Is that why you didn't want that turkey sandwich?"

"No, I'm vegan," he says.

I smile. "Then the meat sandwiches aren't gonna come in handy, are they?"

"No, just kidding. I'm actually nothing," he says. He shrugs. "I mean, no restrictions. Food-wise, religion-wise—"

"Ariel." I feel a tug on my sleeve. *"Ariel."*

I turn slowly and see Zena behind me. "Yes?"

"Give me ten dollars," she says.

I narrow my eyes at her. "For what?"

"This corn pen. Plus this snow globe with the falling corn."

When I look back around, Andre's gone.

When we get ready to leave, Mom has saved me the seat next to her. She has something to say, I can tell.

"Look, we got you something at the doll museum." I'm afraid she's going to hand me a doll, but Mom hands me a postcard. It's cool, but I don't want to tell her that, so I just nod. "Hm. Interesting," I say.

"How about 'thanks,' " she suggests.

"It's just a postcard," I say.

"Ariel."

"Thank you for the postcard, Mother," I say formally.

"What is bothering you?" she asks.

"Besides the fact you didn't tell us we were going on a bus tour with a bunch of senior citizens?"

"What's so wrong with that? I thought you'd be glad to see your grandparents," she says.

"I am, Mom. But weren't we going to visit them for a couple weeks, anyway?"

"Yes, but—"

"Where are we going, exactly? And what's the point?"

"Does there have to be a point? Don't be so rigid," she says. "Not everything in life is neat and tidy. You're so goal-oriented that sometimes you miss out on life."

Yes, I am missing out on life. Right this second, I think, as I look out the window and see an animal that could be a bison off in the distance. That's very cool, seeing a buffalo, and I almost tell her, but I don't want to make her happy by acting happy. Some wild animals that were once nearly extinct won't make up for the fact that we've been essentially kidnapped, all because she wants to get out of town and away from Dad and memories of Dad for a few weeks.

"I'm afraid you're not being open to the journey," she says.

"Mom, it's day two. Are you going to get on my case already?" I ask.

"Well, every day counts," she says, pulling her gray-brown hair back into an ear-of-corn-shaped barrette. It's curly and thick and the barrette barely contains it.

"How about the fact I didn't even know this was the journey we were going on? Does that count?" I ask.

She rummages in her oversize shoulder bag and pulls out a package of cheese sticks, offering me one. "What do you mean?"

"You didn't tell us what we'd be doing, or where we're going, or anything," I say. "Don't you think that was kind of misleading?"

"It was a surprise. A well-intentioned surprise," she says.

"Yeah, but did you think about us?"

"Of course."

"And you thought it'd be okay for me to spend day after day sitting on a bus and having to find time to run like it was an afterthought?" I say.

"Running's important to you. Yes. But it's June, and I thought it wouldn't affect you too much because the season doesn't start until the end of August," she says. "It's not like I planned this trip for August. I could have, I suppose."

"Well, who knows *what* you're planning for August. But you'll probably tell us in August."

There's a long, awkward silence, and then she says, "Speaking of August."

"What?" I ask.

She clears her throat. "We might be moving, actually. In August."

"*Moving?*"

"Sure, why not? Get a fresh start in a new house, a new neighborhood."

"But . . . we *love* our neighborhood. And—Mom. Dylan lives there," I say.

"Yes, well. We're not going to organize our lives around Dylan," she says.

She can be so heartless—and clueless that she's being that way. I'll be having the worst day ever, but instead of noticing, she'll work late helping some client of hers with a new life-coaching plan.

I can hardly believe she's saying this. "Moving. How far?" I ask.

"Maybe only a few miles," she says, sounding nervous. "Maybe more than that."

"I'm not changing schools," I declare. "No way. I'm not leaving Sarah and all my friends."

I can't handle this right now. I stand up and walk down the aisle a few seats. "Uncle Jeff?" I ask. "Could you switch with me? I want to visit with Grandma."

"Oh. Well," he says. He seems a little reluctant to budge.

"We need to talk about girl stuff. And things of that nature," I explain.

"Say no more." Uncle Jeff is up and moving, and I sit down next to Grandma Timmons.

"Hi, there. What's up?" she asks. "Did you want to talk?"

I wrinkle my nose. "Not really. I just needed a change of scenery. Is that okay?"

She nods. "Sometimes it's better just to think things through than to talk all the time about them. Let's play backgammon."

We used to play every summer at their cabin in northern Minnesota. As I set up the mini travel board and swing my checkers into place, I think about how we'd all crowd into that small cabin, and how my dad constantly wanted to play "double or nothing" when it came to backgammon, or gin rummy, or Parcheesi. Then it was quadruple or nothing, and pretty soon we'd be laughing at how many times he could double "double or nothing" without losing track. He'd start with the doubling cube that came with the backgammon set, but when he went past those numbers, he'd stack pennies on the counter, like towering poker chips, to remind him of the score between us on rainy days when we played for hours. One time when he was out of pennies, he used pieces of puffed rice cereal instead— Honey Bears, I think.

"So. How's it going?" Grandma asks as she rolls the dice.

"Fine. But we're not talking, right?" I ask.

"Not at all," she says. "But if you ever wanted to, you could."

"Right."

"But you don't have to."

"No."

"Agreed," she says.

I wonder if I could spell it out somehow in backgammon checkers. SOS.

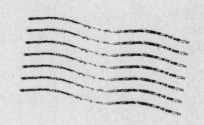

Corn Palace, Mitchell, SD
The one and only corn palace in the world!*

Dylan,
I miss you.
   Corny enough for you?
   I think I just figured out what my next
science/art project will be.
   Wish you were here.
   Is that corny also?
   This place is having an effect on me,
what can I say.
   AF

*That *we* know of!

|...||...||..|.|||....||...||...||...|.|..|.||.|..|.|.....|.||

Chapter Eight

We land at a place called the Horizon Inn for the night.

I don't see much on the horizon, except for days and days in the future spent sitting on a bus. The sun is nowhere near to setting yet, which is nice. We have free time until we all meet for dinner at the attached steakhouse at seven.

I want to go running, but when I look around the parking lot, it seems like there are no roads, just little streets connecting different parking lots.

When we walk into our room, the curtains seem to be made of old, sun-faded striped rugby shirts, and there is a generally musty smell, which reminds me of swampy places we've visited before. I wish I could crack a joke about the place, but I can't think of anything good, and it hits me that what this situation needs is a goofy dad.

One time we stayed at a motel where we lifted up the trash can and found a toad underneath it. My father immortalized it in a journal entry on our trip called "On the Toad, with apologies to Jack Kerouac."

Dad made a cage for the toad out of one of my running shoe boxes and we took it along with us for a day. When the toad died, we buried him at a rest area near Topeka and took a picture with the caption "On Golden Pond in the Sky" and labeled his grave HERE LIES TOAD.

We had a memorial service that a couple other people actually attended. Strange people who lurked on the edge. The kind who might frequent rest areas looking for, I don't know, companionship? The ones who might pull out those "Trucker Dating" flyers, looking for love on all the wrong interstates.

Anyway.

Dad might be completely irresponsible, unreliable, and shady, but he has this goofy side that can be fun, which is something Mom seems to have forgotten. He's not completely evil; he never was.

Now, I try to rifle through the drawers in the desk, but the drawers turn out to be fake. Then I spot a postcard on the bedside table, right above the shelf for the miniature Bible. The postcard features a picture of the hotel in its glory days. Before real beds and TVs with more than ten channels were invented, when nylon sheets were, I guess, okay.

I pick it up and write:

Hey Dad—
We haven't seen any dead toads (or
frogs) (or Frog and Toad) yet, but if we
do I will give them a proper burial.
    We did kill one bird so far, and I've
seen more bugs die on the bus windshield
than I ever knew existed.
    It would drive you nuts.
    So would the Leisure-Lee bus sing-
alongs.
    So don't even wish you were here, because
you wouldn't want to be.
        A

∘ ∘ ∘

"You can't go running by yourself out here," my mother says to me five minutes later, but she doesn't offer to come along, which is fine by me. She makes some phone calls while I'm in the bathroom getting dressed, but I really don't pay attention to her.

However, when I step out of our room onto the cheap-looking rusted balcony, my uncle and grandfather are standing there.

My grandfather is wearing running shorts and a T-shirt that says, GRANDMA'S MARATHON 2002, and looks to be in pretty good shape. Why didn't I know this about him? Or did someone tell me and I forgot?

My uncle, on the other hand, is wearing he-capris, which are his extra-long khaki carpenter shorts, and a T-shirt that says, WE DELIVER FOR YOU. He has Greek fisherman–type leather sandals on his feet, with white tube socks.

It hurts to look at him, and it's not just the sun's reflection off the plate-glass motel window.

"I thought you were on disability," I say, trying to talk him out of it. "Are you supposed to be running? I don't think you're supposed to be running." I don't know CPR.

"I'm perfectly fine," Uncle Jeff says.

"It's not his legs; it's a mental disability," my grandfather chimes in. "Squirrelphobia," he whispers to me.

I notice that Uncle Jeff has a big scar on his shin. "Squirrel?" I point.

"No. Bike accident. Harley days."

I nod. You know how some people have what they call their "glory days" or "halcyon days"? My uncle Jeff has "Harley days."

"I just thought, since you're here, and we're all here, we could exercise together." Uncle Jeff smiles at me, and it's a sweet, honest smile, but is this really supposed to be the positive-male-influence stuff? "And if I can work off some of that weight I gained over the past six months, I'll be in better shape, come what may."

"True enough," Grandpa says.

As we're heading out of the parking lot, I see Andre coming back from a nearby store carrying what looks like a comic book. He waves at me, and I wave back. Then we stop near him, because already my uncle needs to make an adjustment to his sandals. This might be the longest, yet shortest, run I ever go on.

"Going to run to the next stop instead of taking the bus?" Andre asks.

"Hm. Good idea," I say.

He checks out my outfit, my legs, my school team T-shirt. I feel myself getting warm from the attention. "You probably could, couldn't you?" he asks.

"Sure, if they ever told us the next stops," I say.

"So, you run a lot," he comments. "Like . . ."

"Every day," I say. "Or at least six days a week."

"I always thought that people who ran were somehow mixed-up," he says.

I did like him, until now. "Mixed-up? As in . . ."

"Confused. Tortured. Disturbed," he says, but he's smiling at me.

Why is he antagonizing me? What did I do? "Oh really? What makes you say that?"

"I don't know." He shrugs and curls the comic book in his hands. "Running, as a sport, I mean, how much fun can that be? You run and run and you never really *get* anywhere, just back to where you started."

"Runners are different," my grandfather steps up and says. "Runners have a certain inner drive that most ordinary people don't understand." He gives Andre a stare that would kind of make me start running, if I were him. "And they crave solitude."

"So . . . why are you running in a group?" Andre asks with a smile.

"Come on. Let's go," Grandpa says, exasperated with him.

"Well, I have to read this comic book and drink this grape soda. So whatever. I'm sure you'll have a much better time pounding the pavement." He lifts his can as if he's toasting us.

I glare at him. I can't believe my one and only ally just stood there and insulted me. Now what's left? I'm a hundred miles into this trip, and I've got nothing to look forward to.

We head for the streets, and it turns out that my grandfather is actually quite fast, which, again, I should have known, but somehow I didn't. He doesn't get out of breath; in fact I don't even hear him breathing much at all. For a second I wonder if he's still alive, but he must be, because he's still jogging and he has this completely comfortable gait.

My uncle, however, needs to lose about fifty pounds, and get some actual sneakers, and things of that nature. But he keeps chugging along, a few hundred yards behind us, and whenever I turn to check on him, he waves cheerfully back, as if this isn't completely killing him, which I know it must be.

When I run, I think. Usually I fantasize about things. Like things that happened in the past that I wish would have happened differently.

I think about the comment I should have had for the Fox News I-Team when I was unprepared. Instead of "No comment," I should have said, "This really isn't a good time for us, so we appreciate your understanding," or, "No, we didn't know anything about this."

When I stop rewriting the past in my head, I clue in to the fact that Uncle Jeff has caught up with us. He and Grandpa are talking about our possible destinations. Actually, Grandpa's doing most of the talking, while Uncle Jeff huffs and puffs to keep up.

"What do you think, Jeff? Montana? Colorado?"

"Unh," Uncle Jeff grunts.

"We're headed straight west at this point, so of course it's hard to say, and they're known for pulling a switch at the last minute. Or so they claim. They may be all talk, though. I don't trust either one of them," Grandpa says.

Have I been *sleeping* through this first day? Why didn't I realize or pay attention to the fact that we're heading west—farther and farther west, in fact? "Grandpa? If we kept going west from here, where would we end up?" I ask.

"The Pacific Ocean," he says.

I roll my eyes at him. "Before that."

"We'd hit Wyoming first, I guess," he says.

"Yes!" I throw both of my arms in the air.

"What's so exciting about Wyoming?"

"Oh. I, uh, have a friend there I could maybe visit. That's all," I say. "It'd be fun if we, you know, went anywhere close to where he—" I cough. "She lives."

"Mm-hm," says Grandpa. "And how do you figure you'll do that?"

"Bribe Lenny?" I suggest.

Grandpa doesn't look amused, but I don't care. Thanks to him I've just realized that I can ditch this bus trip and find Dylan. I can tell him that no matter what happens, no matter what my mom says? We're not moving in August, or anytime soon.

Or at least, I'm not. Dylan's family can take me in, or I'll live with Sarah.

When I explain these plans to my mother, she'll have only one choice: to decide this moving idea is for the birds. The ugly birds. The pigeons.

When we get back to the motel, I go to the lobby and ask the desk clerk/steakhouse host for a map. I look at where we are, what direction we're headed. If we keep heading west—and why wouldn't we?—we'll hit the Badlands and Mount Rushmore.

It's funny, because my dad always talked about visiting Mount Rushmore—it was always "on the table" with his other trip plans every summer, but we never headed in this direction. He has this list of major things to see, and though we did the Grand Canyon, the Rockies, the Everglades, and New York City, we never made it to

Rushmore. Now I will, and he won't.

I'm walking out to go back to the room and take a shower when Jenny walks in. It's not that hard to corner her by the plate of free beef jerky and cookies on the check-in desk.

"Hey," I say, stopping beside her. "I have a question."

"Sure thing, Zena," she says.

I frown. "Ariel. Anyway. Is it possible you could tell me where we're going in the next couple of days? You know, for the rest of the trip, actually."

"Oh no. You know the Leisure-Lee rules. It's a surprise itinerary. We find that guests have a much better time that way. It gives you the opportunity to relax without being hung up on timetables."

Does she have any idea she's talking to a runner? I'm standing here drenched in sweat, with a sleek Nike sports watch on my wrist, and she's saying that timing yourself is a bad thing. I live for time.

"But does *anyone* know where we're going?" I ask her. "I mean . . . you guys have to know."

Jenny shrugs. "Yes."

"So can you tell me, anyway? Because I *am* hung up on schedules and that kind of stuff. What day would we be at, say, Mount Rushmore?"

Jenny shakes her head and grabs another stale oatmeal raisin cookie, crumbs falling as she lifts it off the paper plate. "Impossible to predict. If we see something we really want to see, we'll spend more time there. We don't have to be anywhere on any particular night."

"But what about hotels? Those must be booked already," I argue. "And our bag lunches? I mean, someone has to make those in advance." Poorly, I might add.

"Well . . . yes," Jenny admits.

"So it can't be totally spontaneous."

She has a tight smile as she looks at me, as if she's considering calling a bus vote to ask me to quit bothering her. "Why is it so important to know everything?"

"I'm just . . . well, see, my training. There's a 10K race at Mount Rushmore on the, uh, twentieth," I improvise.

"A race at the monument?" She laughs. "What do you do, scale the thing? Sounds more like rock climbing than running to me."

Her sense of humor is right up there with her narrating skills.

"It's a race in Rapid City, but it's called the Mount Rushmore Race. So if we're going to be there then, I could run it," I say. Only a real runner will dispute this, and already Jenny's spent time telling us that she's a snorkeler, a volleyball player, and a kayaker. Not a runner. "And I need to run a certain number of races this summer to be, uh, eligible," I tell her. "For a scholarship. Really big deal, this scholarship."

"Really. Well, we'll see. Find out a bit more about the race and we'll let you know."

"But eventually we are going more . . . west?" I ask. "We are going to continue going west?"

"Sure," Jenny says. "We'll see the big things and the small things. And that's all I can tell you right now." She winks at me as if this is amusing tour-guide humor, and then leaves the lobby.

Which is all right, because she was grating on my nerves, plus she ate all the cookies, and I've found out everything I need to. We're heading west.

Which means, theoretically, Wyoming.

Which means I can meet up with Dylan and have this really romantic getaway for a day or two in the middle of this heinous trip. Or maybe I'll get away and I won't go back.

That's what's going to happen on the road: me and Dylan.

Well, not *on* the road, on the road. You know what I mean.

That night after dinner I write Dylan to tell him the good news. I bring his postcard down to the front desk to mail it even though I am in my pajamas, but then I see there's a mailbox outside, on the edge of the parking lot. If I leave it at the front desk, they'll read it; then they'll tell my mom what's on it or something.

How many days on a bus before you become a total raving paranoiac?

When I turn around after slipping the postcard into the mailbox, I see Andre sitting on his balcony. He's listening to his iPod and drinking a soda, and waves to me. He slides off the headphones. "Hey."

"Hey." I wish I were wearing more than my PJs, which consist of a tank top and boxer shorts. "How's that grape soda?" I call up in a whisper.

"It's orange. Cheers," he says as he lifts the can to show it to me.

"Isn't it kind of late?"

"To drink orange soda? Oh gosh. Do you think it will keep me up? I'm sharing a room with my *mother*. Do you understand?"

I laugh. "So am I."

"Yeah, but that's different," he says.

"Oh." I think about it for a second. "I see what you're saying."

"Right."

"Well, at least you have the dog."

We stand there, me with one foot on the balcony steps, him leaning over the railing. I feel like we're in a play. Not *Romeo and Juliet*, something American and Western that's really, really tragic, but without gunplay.

Wait, maybe it would be an Alfred Hitchcock movie. *Strangers on a Bus*.

"I still have four quarters," Andre says. "You want something from the vending machine?"

I'm about to say no when I realize that saying no means going back to my room, where Zena and Grandma are dyeing Mom's hair to make her look younger. They won't miss me for a while yet, and I won't miss them.

"Sure." He goes down the balcony to the machine, while I climb the steps, thankful for flip-flops. There are a couple of white plastic chairs, so I sit in one.

Andre comes back and holds out a can. "This is what they had."

I get a Dr. Stepper, which is apparently a knockoff brand, with an image of someone doing aerobics.

"Hey, you could be drinking this. Scorange." He holds it up and I see a giant soccer ball image on the can. "It's like some sports drink gone berserk. Mad. Insane. Over the edge."

"Quietly, leisurely crazy," I add.

We sit there for a while. "So, you have other plans for the summer?" he asks.

"Oh yeah. Lots." I sip the black-cherry soda, which is pretty far from being a sports drink.

"Me too."

We stare at the steady line of eighteen-wheelers pulling into the truck stop across the road.

"I was thinking. We're heading west, right?"

I smile. "Right."

"Well, my dad lives in California. I'm going to go there instead."

"Instead? How?"

He points across the divided highway at the truck stop. "They'd drive all night. Straight through, probably. Get us there in the morning."

Us? I think. Does he mean me, or the trucker? "You wouldn't actually do that. Would you?" Never mind the fact that I think his sense of time and distance is off.

"Catch a ride with a truck that's headed there? Why not?"

"Because bad things happen in trucks. You're too young."

"Am not."

"Only people who are too young say things like 'am not,'" I point out.

He laughs. "So what about you? You going to stay on the bus?"

"I guess it depends where we go."

"Yeah, I guess so. So why don't we find out?" He gets to his feet and starts walking away toward the stairs.

"How?" I ask, getting up to follow him.

"The bus, how else?"

"We can't break into the bus," I say.

"Why not?" Andre glances over his shoulder as we walk around to where the bus is parked.

"Because!" I reach out and grab his arm. "Lenny and Jenny. They probably sleep on the bus."

"Why would they do that?"

"I don't know. They're devoted to Leisure-Lee?"

"You're crazy."

"Not as crazy as you, obviously."

Andre tries to pull open the bus door, but it doesn't even give an inch. He grabs a stick from the ground and wedges it into the tiny opening, pushing and maneuvering until the stick breaks in two, flies off, and hits a nearby car.

Just then I see Lenny walking across the parking lot toward us. "Oops," I whisper.

"Does he have a bus-cam hooked up to his room or something?"

Andre asks under his breath.

"What's going on, mates?" Lenny asks.

"Oh! I, uh, left something on the bus," Andre says.

"What's that then? Your ee-pod." Lenny chuckles.

"Right. My ee-pod," Andre says. "No, actually it's a book. It must have slipped out of my backpack, and I need it in order to fall asleep, so I didn't want to disturb anyone—"

"Say no more. Not a problem." Lenny unlocks the door and Andre gets on, hunting around for something. I climb up the steps halfway and peer around the driver's seat, looking for a map or any kind of clue, but the area is so cluttered with papers that I wouldn't know where to start.

"How's Chuckles?" Lenny calls from behind me.

"Cuddles, you mean?" Andre asks as he roots around underneath his seat.

"Fine. Sleeping soundly."

"Did he like the steak scraps we sent up?" asks Lenny.

"Loved 'em," Andre says, his voice muffled as he crawls around. "You know what? I can't find it. It must be in my mom's bag somewhere—she's got so much stuff in there, you need a flashlight."

When we step off the bus, Mom is wandering around the parking lot, calling my name. I call to her and wave.

Her hair is under plastic wrap, coated in white liquid. "*There* you are. You had us worried sick!" she says, hurrying over.

"I'd worry more about those chemicals on your head," I say, backing up from the strong smell.

"I'm going Mysterious Auburn Brown. With blond highlights," she adds.

"Those might be the only highlights on this trip," I murmur as I follow her back to our room.

The Horizon Inn & Steak House.
Eat like a man, sleep like a baby. Convenient to interstate.
Early check-in; late checkout available. Charges apply.

Dylan—
You won't believe this, but I think we're heading to Wyoming, or at least really close! Not sure when we'll get there, but in a week or so maybe.
Can you believe it?
I'll let you know details when we're getting closer so we can hook up.
Can't wait to see u!!!
Ariel

ı.,.ıll,.,.ıl,.ı.ıllı..,.ıl,..,ıl..ıl,.,.ı.ı.ı,ılı.ı.ıbı..,.l.ıll

Chapter Nine

"*You* are a sweetheart. I can tell just by looking at you," Andre's mother says the next morning. She gives me a little hug as we stand in line to board the bus.

"I am?" I wonder out loud.

"For sure." Mrs. O'Neill is wearing a sleek black wrap shirt and jeans, with stylish high-heeled black sandals. A large black-and-pink-striped handbag over her arm contains the infamous Cuddles, whose collar matches the bag. "Your hair looks great, Tamara. I can't get over it. You look ten years younger."

"Really? You think so, Lorraine?"

Mom's hair is dark brown, with a few gray and blond streaks. I'm not sure what's mysteriously auburn about it. She's wearing a pair of gold corn earrings and a bright gold Corn Palace sweatshirt. That doesn't help matters.

"Definitely. Isn't this a great trip?" Andre's mother asks me, and I smile.

"It's not horrible," I say, with a tight-lipped smile at my mother.

"Is that the best you can say, honey?" Mrs. O'Neill asks.

"For now. Pretty much." I nod.

"Mm-hm. You sound just like Andre. You two need to get into the traveling mood, get your traveling shoes on."

Andre glances down at my green-and-white-striped vintage running shoes. "I think she's ready, Ma. See you."

Mom puts her hand on my arm. "Actually—hold up. I was thinking we should sit together, Ariel."

"Nonsense. You and I have *lots* more in common, Tamara," says Lorraine. "I want to talk, not sit and listen to Andre's music."

Now I'm the one who wants to hug *her*.

Andre and I leave our moms to enjoy each other and sit down in the third row again, scrunching down in our seats together. I've decided to forgive his running insult. I can't afford to antagonize the only peer I have on the bus, even if he already antagonized me. I think about our escapade the night before, wonder if Lenny is suspicious of us at all. I stretch out, recline the seat back a little bit.

Lenny finishes taking roll and climbs onto the bus. Jenny follows him, and soon we're pulling out of the parking lot, back onto the highway. Lenny leads everyone in his so-called eye-opening routine, which is a goofy song. This morning it's "If You're Happy and You Know It."

"Do you think Lenny caught on last night?" I ask Andre while everyone's singing and clapping hands.

"No. Not at all," Andre says.

"So should we try again?" I ask. "I'd really like to know where we're going. I hate this crap about everything being a surprise. We do road trips like this every summer, but before now I always knew what the destination was, what the *plan* was," I say.

His eyebrows shoot up. "Wow. No wonder."

"No wonder what?"

"You don't seem as traumatized as I do because you've done this before."

I laugh. "No, but—see, I am. Because we usually do the traveling in our car, not on a bus, and usually our dad comes along, and it's a lot more fun." Of course, I didn't always think so at the time, but in retrospect those trips were probably the most fun we ever had together as a family.

"Still. You don't seem totally upset," he comments.

"I hide things really well," I say.

He nods. "So when you want to kill me, I won't see it coming."

"Not at all," I promise.

"Damn. That's going to be tough." He opens his vocabulary book and starts highlighting. "So. Where's your dad this summer?"

"He's . . . uh . . . home," I say with an awkward nod. I give a nervous laugh, feeling like I want to both tell him the entire sordid story, and crawl under the seat and go sit with my grandmother for a while and not talk about it at all.

I've been going to a counselor ever since my dad developed this gambling "problem," plus family therapy, and it helps some things, but it doesn't help others. Like, I don't really want to talk to other people and tell them what happened, even if it's in the middle of nowhere and I'll never see this person again after we get off this bus.

"My mom and dad split up over the holidays," I explain. That's nice and vague.

"So did mine," Andre says.

"What a coincid—"

"Ten years ago," he adds.

"Oh." I give an embarrassed, shoot-me-now smile.

"It's okay, I'm sort of over it," he says. "He moved to California. He sends money, and I visit a couple times a year. It's a 'quality relationship.' " He makes quotation marks with his fingers.

"My mom's the queen of 'quality relationships,' " I say, echoing his quotes. "Not having one. Just talking about it." I lean closer and whisper, "My uncle and grandfather are here to be positive male influences for me. Okay, so. My grandpa is totally miserable to be here—he didn't want to come, he didn't even want to retire, but my grandma insisted, because she wanted to take trips together. And the other one, my uncle Jeff, is so upbeat I don't believe a word he says because it all sounds fake. You know?"

"Positive's overrated." He sighs. "But I'm pretty sure this positively sucks."

I laugh, while he goes back to his vocabulary book, and I take out my stack of postcards, a few other things, and some art supplies I've collected. Lenny is talking about the geology of the area, and how we're headed for a fascinating little corner of the world known as Wall and we'll be there for a Leisure-Lee lunch. And every time I glance out the window I see a billboard for a place called Wall Drug.

I've picked up scraps from brochures, tickets, and receipts. I bought rubber cement at the last drugstore of choice (being a bus full of senior citizens we stop at a lot of drugstores) and I start pasting words and photos on top of the plain white prestamped postcards my grandmother gave me.

After I've done a few, Andre asks, "What are you, scrapbooking?"

"I guess," I say. "But not exactly."

"My mom does that. Or used to, anyway. I called it crapbooking. Yours looks cooler, though. When did you start doing that?" he asks.

"I don't know," I admit. "I guess about six months ago."

Over Christmas break when everything came to light—that there were no presents, that Dad had spent everything in the bank and then some—Mom signed up me and Zena for about twelve thousand activities to keep us busy. Art classes like Painting and Creative Memories. Gymnastics. Swimming lessons. Diving lessons. At one point she even suggested synchronized swimming and diving as a way to get me and Zena to become better friends. Which was funny, because neither Zena nor I like to swim all that much, and we can't stand each other half the time, so why would we dive together?

Anyway, all these classes were supposed to take our minds off the fact that they were getting the fastest "trial separation" in the history of Milwaukee, that Dad was moving back home with his parents, that Dad might be going *on* trial.

Pretty much the only thing I got out of it was the idea of making stuff by using found objects.

"Huh. It's good. Who's Gloves?" Andre asks a minute later.

I frown at him, because I thought he was busy writing something of his own. "Not that you're reading what I'm writing or anything. But she's my cat."

He lowers his glasses and looks me in the eye. "You're writing to your cat. That's pathetic. Desperate."

"You forgot needy," I add.

"That too," he says. "Your cat is named Gloves?"

I shrug. "She was named Mittens until I found out that was really common, so I renamed her. She has white paws, but the rest of her is black, except for this white patch over her eyes."

"That must get in the way of her reading your postcards," Andre comments.

"Shut up," I say, laughing. "Okay, so I guess basically this is for my grandmother. My other grandmother. The one who's not in seat twelve-B."

He laughs. "You're funny. The thing is, uh, maybe we should get something out in the open. Being, you know, on the open road and all."

"Okay," I say slowly, wondering what this is about.

"I don't really want to like you. Is that okay?"

I don't know what to say to that, so I sit there waiting for him to make sense, to say it three different ways.

"I'm not looking for . . . you know. A girlfriend. A mate. A—"

"Okay, fine," I interrupt. "I get it. Neither am I. I'm not looking for a mate or whatever. I'm already seeing someone, anyway." Sort of.

"Oh, you are?"

"Well, yeah."

"How come he's not on the bus? Or wait. It's not Dieter, is it?" he asks as he looks back at the German twins.

I just glare at him.

"Okay, so it's not Dieter." He pauses. "Is it Wolfgang?"

"His name's Dylan," I say.

"How uncommon," he says dryly.

"Look, are you going to mock everything I say?"

"Probably," he admits. "So where's the infamous Dylan?"

"He's at camp in Wyoming. Here." I pull out our impromptu prom photo, the one Sarah took when she saw me and Dylan leaving prom together. I show it to Andre, feeling kind of stupid as I do, as if I have to offer up proof.

Andre narrows his eyes as he stares at the picture. "Isn't he a little old for summer camp?" he asks.

"He's a counselor. Obviously." I try not to laugh, but it's impossible. "Quit making fun of him, okay?" I say.

"Why? He's not here; it's not like he'll know."

"Yeah, but I will, and then I'll have to dislike you," I say.

He looks at me as if he's thinking of saying something. But he holds back. He goes back to his vocabulary book and highlighter pen. "These little seat-back tables are the perfect height; have you noticed?"

We sit there and I work on doctoring a postcard while he studies words. His highlighting is annoying. "Are you going for spelling champ or something?" I ask.

"Whatever they'll give me." He hunches over the book, screening me out. And over the CD soundtrack to *Oklahoma!*, which Lenny and Jenny love to play, I just hear the *screech, screech* of a smelly orange highlighter.

"If you ever finish any of those pages, like, don't need them? Can I have them?"

He flips through the book and rips out a page. "Here. I'm done with the As."

I look at the page.

aromatic

asymptomatic

axiomatic

"Thanks." Then I rip off the one I can define and paste it onto a postcard. "You know what's weird about postcards? When you're used to IMs, postcards are long, slow, and totally unsatisfying. You get, like, *no* response."

"I'd write back to you," Andre says. "Immediately. Instantaneously. At once."

"You would?"

"I would."

"How?"

He thinks it over for a second. "Carrier pigeon?" he suggests.

"The thing is . . . Ariel. Um, I already have a girlfriend," he says. "A skirt. Arm candy. You know."

I stare at him in horror. "You don't actually talk like that, do you?"

"What?"

"Calling her arm candy. That's disgusting," I say.

He laughs. "Yeah. Maybe that's why she moved to Denver."

"No wonder."

"We're still friends, though. So if we don't hit California, maybe we'll hit Denver, and I can call her. We could probably stay with her awhile."

"Sure," I say, wondering when I became part of his escape plan. Apparently I'm not the only one on the bus with a big fantasy life. "But if I go anywhere, it'll be to Wyoming." And then the bus suddenly makes this loud bang and lurches to the side of the road.

The tiny chipmunk is easy prey for a red-tailed hawk in the
early-morning light.

Dear Gloves,
I ran into a friend of yours today. Okay,
not a "friend." A "meal," once. Or did you
just toy with it until it escaped? I can't
remember.
    Remember when Zena used to say "chickmunk"
instead of "chipmunk"?
    She has a gift for making up words, like
the rest of our clan.
    She's twelcreative.
    Miss u.
    P.S. Why do photographers just take pictures
of these killings, and not stop them? Hello?
ASPCA?

I,..II,..II.,I.III...II,..iII...II...I.I..I,II.I..I.I...I.II

Sarah,

Met this guy on the bus.

I won't say much else about him because he'll read it over my shoulder.

In fact he's probably doing that now.

He actually referred to his ex as "arm candy." Is that disgusting or what?

Yes, you, Andre. You're disgusting.

Hope you're meeting better guys at your summer job.

At least you have more than one to choose from.

Xo

A

Chapter Ten

Jenny manages to steer the bus onto an exit ramp, but from there things don't look promising. Whenever she tries to restart the engine, it kicks on for a minute, then dies again, so we just pathetically coast until we're in the parking lot of a place called the Wild Wilde West. Complete with wooden fence surrounding the Wild Wilde West Museum, the Wild Wilde West Gift Shoppe, and the Wild Wilde West Sculpture Garden.

Lenny gets to his feet, turns, and faces us, while Jenny scrambles out the door frantically.

"Well, this wasn't on the itinerary, now, was it?" Lenny smiles at all of us and coughs nervously. "And, uh, it's little gems like this place that you'll remember about the trip. Not the big stuff, mates." Lenny winks at us. "The small stuff."

"Like the bus maintenance record," my grandfather mutters, standing behind me in the aisle.

"We won't remember Mount Rushmore, but we'll remember this?" I turn around and ask him.

"In the way that bad memories often outlive good ones," he says, and we both smile—dejected smiles, but still.

"Everybody off, have a look around. This looks to be a fun spot. Right, then. We'll fix the bus and be back on the road pronto. And then we'll . . ." Lenny pauses.

"Hit Wall!" a few older tourists yell.

Lenny makes a clicking noise with his tongue. "Exactamundo." Then he shuts off his microphone and opens the door for all of us.

When I step outside, it's like walking into a wall of heat. "Wall" being the word of the day. "How did it get so hot? How is it possible?" I ask.

"Well, it's like this," Uncle Jeff says, and he starts to talk about weather, which I guess he knows a lot about, having to deliver the mail, no matter what.

"Mom, aren't you so hot in that sweatshirt?" I ask.

"Thank you." She takes a bow.

I look around for Andre, hoping for sympathy, but he's busy arguing with his mom about who's going to stay outside and watch Cuddles, because the dog's not allowed inside. I walk around the end of the bus and there are Lenny and Jenny in the middle of an argument.

"You should let me drive for a while," Lenny says.

"It's not the driver, you moron," Jenny says.

"Oh, isn't it just," Lenny replies. "And what did you call me?"

Maybe the heat is getting to them, I think. They have one of those relationships that you don't necessarily want to spend much time around, if you can help it.

I wander into the Wilde Museum and find out I'm the last person in, as the entire bus population presses into the small lobby. It turns out we're in time for the eleven a.m. tour of the Wild Wilde West, which is dedicated to the writer Oscar Wilde.

The tour consists of a bunch of stuff about Oscar Wilde, with hardly any connection to this place or to the West at all. Mom is laughing hysterically at all the Oscar Wilde puns and memorabilia, and the slightly-over-the-top-in-five-different-ways tour guide's attempt to claim that "Oscar Wilde Slept Here." If he did, does that really matter to us? And why would he? Did his tour bus break down, too?

"Poor Oscar Wilde," my grandfather mutters to me as the museum guide rambles on excitedly.

"No doubt," I agree. I don't know much about him, but my friend Sarah was in the play *The Importance of Being Earnest* in summer theater, so I saw it four or five times.

There's a wooden set piece here, a photo thing with a circle cut out for you to stick your head into, and you pose next to Oscar Wilde in chaps, and there's some line about if you have your photo taken here—for $19.95—you will not age, just like Dorian Gray in *The Picture of Dorian Gray*, which I unfortunately read last summer when I was bored and found it on my mother's bookshelf.

Andre comes up behind me, smuggling in Cuddles, who's tucked under his arm. "He was gay, right, but does that mean he wore chaps?" he asks.

"He also wore fur." I point at a photo of Oscar Wilde with a fur collar on his winter coat. "Does that make him Western?"

"No, but it makes him eligible to be hated by PETA," he says.

"Are these rhetorical questions? And if so, can anyone join in?" my mom asks.

We sort of edge away from her, without answering, toward the exit at the back, which leads out to the so-called sculptures. "Does wearing a dead animal make you a Western hero?" I ask.

"Do you think he actually slept here, or he just passed out here from the heat?" Andre says.

We stand in the doorway. There are five little cars sticking into the ground, their hoods buried in the sandy earth. Nose first, as if they fell from the sky.

Andre sets down Cuddles, who's on the world's smallest, shortest leash. Cuddles immediately runs over to one of the buried cars and pees on the tires.

"You've heard of Carhenge?" the museum guide asks us, stepping onto the back deck behind us.

"No," Andre says.

The guide points to Cuddles. "Is that your dog?"

"No," Andre says again.

"Totally cute," the guide comments. "I have a teacup poodle. Anyway, Carhenge is in Nebraska. It's made of vintage cars, and it's a replica of Stonehenge. You know, the mysterious, ancient circle of stones."

"We *know* what Stonehenge is," Andre says with a bored sigh.

"Well, this is Mini Carhenge. Because it's made of Mini Coopers. Get it?" He laughs.

We stand back and look at his miniature car circle. Only it's a semicircle, if that, and they're all the same height. "But that doesn't look like Stonehenge at all," Andre observes.

"I know. It's totally cuter," the guide says. "That's the point. It's a miniature version."

"Interesting. We should see if Lenny and Jenny will take us to Carhenge," Andre says. "I mean, we do have this loose itinerary and all."

"Oh, you really should go. It's magnificent," the guide says. "Breathtaking."

"Hm. Well, we'll just have a look around, take some photos," Andre tells him, and we step off.

"Don't forget your Wilde souvenir shopping," the guide says. "Plenty of mini mementos inside!"

"Right," Andre says. And he makes that little clicking noise that Lenny has started to make, with little gun gestures. "Exactamundo."

A tumbleweed blows across the half-dirt, half-grass surface, and Cuddles barks, charging at it in full-on Chihuahua attack mode.

Five minutes later Uncle Jeff comes outside and insists on taking our picture posing against the Mini cars, with Cuddles on top of one of them, except that the car is too hot and it slightly burns Cuddles's tender feet.

"A mini dog on a mini car," Uncle Jeff says. "Oh, this is fantaster-rific. The guys back home will love this. And when I say guys, I don't mean just guys; I mean people. Other letter carriers. We covered that in gender-sensitivity training."

"I have to get out of here," Andre says out of the side of his mouth as we pose for the tenth picture. "When do we mutiny, exactly?"

I look over my shoulder at him.

"Mutiny. A noun. Revolt. Coup," Andre says robotically.

"I know what it *means*," I say. Maybe he's not studying for tests, but if I stick around him long enough, I should be ready for anything. "Do you just assume you have to define every word with synonyms for the rest of the world?"

"Not the rest of the world. Just you," he says.

"Shut up."

"Seriously," he says.

"Yes. Seriously, shut up," I say.

We finish our photo shoot and walk around the side of the building, where we discover Jenny and Lenny arguing about what's wrong with the bus.

"We're not going to make Wall," Lenny is saying. "And this place, charming as it is, doesn't have a snack bar. Unless you consider Cadbury bars a lunch option."

"He said there's a pizza place in town. We'll have to get pizzas delivered," Jenny says.

Lenny shakes his head. "Lee told us no extra expenses."

"Lee? Why are you bringing up Lee? Are you trying to give me a heart attack?" Jenny asks. "The bus breaks down, that's bad enough. Lee's going to kill us."

"Exactamundo," Lenny says.

"Quit saying that already, or *I'm* going to kill you," Jenny threatens. "This is a disaster."

"Accidents happen, mate. We'll be fine."

"How can you be so relaxed? I hate that about you," Jenny says.

"And how can you be so uptight all the time?" Lenny replies.

Andre and I look at each other. "Things are taking an interesting turn," he comments. "Look at it this way. They fight some more, they turn against each other—they're vulnerable. Divide and conquer. Then we can make our move."

"What's our move?" I ask.

He shrugs and picks up Cuddles, who's whining a little bit. "Busjack? Is that even a word?"

To kill time while we wait, I go running. I'm already wearing clothes that'll work for a short run, but I go over to the bus to grab my real running shoes because I don't want to wreck my arches in my vintage suede Sauconys. As I tie the laces, I make sure Jenny sees me, so she'll buy into my plan of needing to be somewhere on a specific date for a specific run.

Grandpa comes with me, and so does Uncle Jeff, and to my surprise

Andre kicks into stride beside me. "What the hell?" he says. "What else am I going to do—buy and read an Oscar Wilde novel?" He starts breathing a little more heavily. "Wait a second. I think I will. See you."

He drops off, just like that. When I glance back at him, I see that behind me a trail of power-walking seniors, half wearing sun visors, has formed. We're going up and down the road as if we're on leave from a psychiatric hospital.

About half a mile down the road I hear a squeal behind us and turn to see my uncle sprinting at top speed in our direction.

"Squirrel—" he manages to get out. And he's moving so fast that I can't quite believe it's him running toward me.

"Jeff. Jeff, calm down. That was a prairie dog," my grandfather tells him.

"Oh." He's panting and panting, sounding sort of like a dog. And as soon as he reaches us he stops running. So we do, too. Then my grandfather lifts his water bottle and squirts cold water in his face.

"Snap out of it," he says. "A squirrel can't hurt you. Neither can a prairie dog."

"Well." Uncle Jeff clears his throat. "You never know how animals will act when they're threatened, and things of that nature."

"Prairie dogs don't bite," my grandfather argues.

"Have you ever had a rabies shot?" my uncle shoots back.

"Come on, Uncle Jeff, let's do a cool-down jog, so your muscles don't get tight," I say, and the three of us start moving again. "How are the, uh, shoes?"

"I think I'd better invest in some new ones," he says, glancing down at the leather sandals wearing a welt into the top of his foot.

When I get back from running, Mom is standing there cursing at the bus. "Damnit, damnit."

It's completely understandable, so I don't even know why I bother to ask, "What's wrong? Besides the obvious." I wipe my forehead with the bottom of my sleeveless T-shirt.

"I lost my ring, my wedding band," she says.

"What? How?"

"I bought this lotion inside. It was a joke gift for Marta; it's this Dorian Gray Forever Young Beauty Lotion, and I was trying it out, rubbing it on my hands, and it was so slick and greasy that my ring fell off and it rolled under the bus. Now I can't see it anywhere."

There's an awkward pause, and then she swears again. "Damnit, damnit, damnit," she keeps muttering, and then she starts crying.

"Don't worry, we'll find it," I tell her. "And, Mom, I'm not saying this to be mean, but . . . you're not married anymore," I say. "So, do you honestly still need the ring?"

"I know. I *know*," she says, anger in her voice. "But if you knew how many times I almost pawned that stupid thing when we were broke, and now it's lost, and I'm upset, and I don't *want* to be upset on my vacation."

"So why don't you let it go?" I ask. "That would be a realsimple way of looking at it. Leave it here."

"No. I couldn't leave it here—to get flattened in a parking lot when this bus finally moves again?" She's horrified by my suggestion.

"Why not? I mean, you're all about closure, right? What could be better than an abandoned ring getting crushed by a—"

"Ariel. Honestly. I don't want it to be ob-obliterated," she stammers. "The ring is part of my history, my life, and it's also about you guys. Your father and I made a commitment to be—to have—a family. We're still a family."

"Of course we're still a family," I say. As angry as she makes me sometimes, I don't enjoy seeing her this upset. "Of course we are.

Except that you keep trying to push Dad out of it, but—"

"He *is* out of it," she argues. "And it's entirely his fault that he is."

"He made a mistake. A big mistake. But he's . . . you know. Still the same guy. Still Dad."

"Would *you* trust him again?" she asks me with a sob, and I have to really think about it, not like I haven't thought about it before, but some days I say yes, and some days I say no. How do you balance someone's entire life against a yearlong streak of disasters?

Before I can say anything, my grandmother, who's just returned from a walk with Zena and Bethany, comes over to Mom and hugs her. "What's wrong?" she asks.

"My ring," she starts to explain.

I get on my belly and crawl partway underneath the bus looking for her stupid wedding ring. I run my hand over the pavement as far as it will go, but all I come up with is gravel. Suddenly there are purple sparkly flip-flops beside my head.

"*Why* were you yelling at Mom? Don't do that," Zena says.

"I wasn't yelling at her," I say, getting to my feet.

"You were," Zena argues. "And she was crying."

"You have no idea, okay?" I tell her. "You don't know everything that's going on."

"I don't? I think maybe *you* have no idea," she replies.

"Zena, please. You're twelve. You're naive. There's stuff you don't understand."

She looks at me as if I should crawl back under the bus and wait for it to drive off. "I understand everything. I've been there for Mom, while you're always running or out with Dylan or Sarah or whoever."

"Oh yeah? So she tells you everything."

Zena shrugs. "Enough, anyway."

"Well, did she tell you she's thinking about us moving?" I say.

And Zena's right eyebrow kind of twitches. "Moving? When?"

"August. She's not telling us where, just like she didn't tell us about this trip, okay? So if Dad kept secrets, he's not the only one."

Zena takes a beat to compose herself. "If we're moving, it's her business, it's her job and her house, and she'd consult us anyway before she did that." Then she turns away from me. "Mom? *Are* we moving?" she asks.

"Go ahead, tell her," I urge Mom.

My grandmother clears her throat and turns to me. "Honey, you look awful. You really ought to clean up. Come on, let's go inside."

She's right. I'm sweating from my run, my shirt is wet, and now it's covered in dirt, twigs, and gravel. I convince Jenny to let me get my duffel out of the luggage bay, and go inside to change.

"Please don't talk about it," I say to Grandma when she follows me into the restroom. "I'm so sick of talking about it."

"I wasn't going to," she says. "I told you, I don't believe in talking until you're blue in the face."

She watches while I rinse my face and arms off with cold water; then she hands me my clothes over the stall door to change into. When I come out, she insists on putting these cute doll barrettes in my hair. "I don't think so," I tell her.

"Just try it. Don't be such a stick-in-the-mud," she says.

"Me?"

"Yes, you."

"You know I'm sixteen, right?" I ask, looking at my reflection, which is kind of like someone trying to dress ten years younger than they are.

"Right, I know," she says. "But if you're sixteen, that means your mother is forty-four, which means I'm sixty-seven. I can't handle that. So let's just pretend for a second that you're not sixteen."

"Okay," I say. "Can I be eighteen?"

She laughs. "Definitely not. Ever."

When we come outside, there are feet sticking out from underneath the bus, and seconds later Wolfgang emerges, holding Mom's wedding ring. She hugs him and knocks off his glasses with her new Wilde cowboy hat.

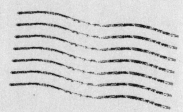

The Wild Wilde West: the only museum in South Dakota dedicated to Oscar Wilde, where you'll go Wilde discovering the Importance of Being Outwest.

Hi Dad,

How is your summer going?

It's really hot here in South Dakota.

I think we're going to Mount Rushmore. We always wanted to see Rushmore, remember?

But the bus is broken down, so at the rate we're going, we might be back home by September. Of next year.

Zena says hi.

Miss you. Wish you were here.

—A

I...II...II.I.III...II...iII...II..I.I.I.II.I..I.I...I.II

Chapter Eleven

We sit outside the museum in the baking sun, eating hot pizza, while a mechanic works to repair the bus.

Lenny is playing a trivia game called Name the Presidents with some people, while others are playing bridge, and still others, finished with their lunches, are napping.

"Let's play Leisure-Lee Fear Factor. South Dakota edition," Andre says.

"Is there any other?" I ask.

Zena and Bethany are doing karaoke, with no machine, using pop straws for mikes. Wolfgang and Dieter ask if they can have a turn, and Wolfgang starts singing "SexyBack," and Dieter does a kind of robotic dance to the sort of drumbeat he's making with his mouth. When they say "VIP," it sounds like *Fee I Pee*.

Dieter's hair looks like Justin Timberlake's. But that's about it.

"They're German rappers. Gerappers," I say to Andre.

"I hate Justin Timberlake songs." Andre points to a plastic container.

"If you drink that garlic dipping sauce in one shot, I'll give you a hundred dollars."

It sounds like the kind of bet my dad would make, then lose. "You're not serious."

He shrugs. "Sure."

"A hundred dollars. Do you really have a hundred dollars to give me when I do it?" I ask.

"You're not going to do it. Because I have to get back on the bus with you, and I don't want you puking. But anyway, why wouldn't I?"

"Sorry. Just assuming your mom is as chintzy as mine," I say. "You say you have it, you have it." How do I know he's not carrying around forgive-me bribes from his father, too? I peel back the top and look inside the cup of dipping sauce. "No, I can't drink it. It's disgusting."

"Good, because I don't actually have the hundred. I have a ten. Want to sip it for ten?" he asks.

"God, no." I glance at the ingredients on the package, which all sound very nauseating. "I actually do have a hundred dollars. It's like . . . blood money, or whatever that phrase is."

"Blood money? You mean, like, tainted, illegal, wrongly gotten?"

He just described my dad and his finances in four words. "Maybe."

"So why not spend it right away?" Andre suggests. "Get rid of it."

"I don't know." I push a slice of pepperoni around on my plate. "I guess because I'm saving it, just in case."

"In case of what?" asks Andre.

I think: *In case he asks for it back when he's broke.* But that's too personal and weird for someone I just met. "Just in case," I say.

He nods. "Good plan." He leans back and looks around at the motley group of pizza eaters. "You know, everyone's pretty distracted right now. It wouldn't be hard to slip off."

I point out that we're in the middle of nowhere, that getting a ride out of here seems impossible, that it'd mean walking down a long, dusty highway. And dying of thirst. Nobody's been at this museum, except us, in the past couple hours. It's obviously not on the list of South Dakota must-sees.

"Okay, so maybe I'll dig out one of those Mini cars. Think they still run?"

"That depends. Did you take auto mechanics in school?"

Andre sighs. "Sometimes we don't know what courses to take until it's too late. You know?"

"Do I ever." When I look over at the road, there's a silvery shimmering wave coming off it. It's kind of the way my head feels. "Are you serious about this mutinous escape plan?" I ask.

"Yes. Up here, anyway." He taps his forehead. "Maybe it's just the garlic talking, but I can't see sticking around when life is actually happening somewhere else."

"Exactly," I say. "And nothing against this store—though it's a little weird—"

"A little?"

"Or these car sculptures—also weird—or the state. It's a fabulous state, and being from big Midwestern states ourselves, we can appreciate the bigness, and the stateness, and the fabulous tourist attractions."

"Definitely," says Andre. "Because we've gone on trips to see Paul Bunyan and Babe the Blue Ox before."

"You have?" I ask.

"Sure."

"Which one? Bemidji, Minnesota, Paul Bunyan, because I've seen that, or Brainerd—"

"How should I know? I was, like, seven," he says. "Anyway, it's not

South Dakota. Maybe I would have rather gone to New York or L.A., but whatever. It's the fact that we're on a bus and, like, nobody is on a bus anymore. And when I have to talk about my summer vacation, I'll have to say I took a trip on a bus. With forty senior cits."

"Is that so bad? The stigma or whatever?"

"When you go to a private school? Yeah. Pretty much."

"Oh."

"People take trips on yachts. Ocean journeys. They go see the Tour de France. And while they're at it, the rest of Europe," he explains. "We're not supposed to be here. I mean, look around. Everyone else here is at least sixty. Or German. Or your sister."

I laugh. "You know what I hate? They say the trip is all about *us*. But it's so not about us. You know?"

Lenny is making a tour of the captives and he stops in front of us. "How are you two enjoying our little detour?"

"Fine," I say.

"Great," says Andre. "What's next?"

"Well. I shouldn't tell you, but . . ." He looks to one side and then the other. "As soon as the bus is fixed, we're traveling up the road a bit. Heading north."

"I thought we were going to Wall," I say. "West. Can we keep going west, please?"

"Nonsense. There's a lovely little café where we've got dinner reservations. Best biscuits and gravy in the entire world, I'm telling you."

"We just had lunch."

"Well, we're not going straight there, of course not. This afternoon we'll be visiting one of the world's largest balls of twine. What is it, second-largest?" he asks Jenny, who's come up beside him.

"I can't believe you're telling them this," she says. "What happened to the element of surprise?"

"They can keep it to themselves. Can't you?" says Lenny.

"Definitely," I tell him.

Jenny eyes me suspiciously. "Anyway," she says. "Leonard, it's not a ball of twine. It's a ball of *yarn*. It's in the Knitting Hall of Fame."

"Twine, yarn, same thing."

"Not the same thing."

"Why do you always have to contradict me?"

"I don't!" says Jenny.

"There. See? You just did it again."

"I did not. Maybe you should ride in the back for a while. Visit with the passengers in the back rows."

"Maybe I will," he replies.

My mom should give them one of her books, or schedule an emergency session. Never mind the bus—I don't think their relationship is going to make it to Wall.

Yarn it all—come back! You've just missed the world's third-largest ball of yarn!

Gloves,
You could have a field day with this thing.
 Miss you,
 A

l...ll...ll.l.lll...dl...ll...ll..l.l..l.ll.l.l.l.....l.ll

Chapter Twelve

The next day, we don't get to Wall until late afternoon. Our off-course adventure ended up taking a very long time because it turned out there had been a mistake (which made Lenny and Jenny argue even more) and we had no motel reservation. So we had to keep driving farther and farther off the beaten path to find a place with enough rooms for all of us. By that time we were practically in North Dakota, or perhaps Canada—I took a long nap and quit paying attention—but Lenny assures us that now we're back on track.

"You've seen the bumper stickers," Lenny says as we pull into a small town with old storefronts that could be real, or could be a movie set or one of those new shopping mall styles. It's really difficult to tell. "You've seen the billboards. Now, experience it for yourselves. Are you ready, guys? Are you ready? Then let's . . . hit Wall!" He pumps his fist in the air as half the people on the bus scream, "Hit Wall!" with him.

There's a story about how Wall Drug began as a place to stop on the older highway: They had a sign up that they offered free ice water to everyone passing by. Now they have a sign up that says their Western Art Gallery restaurant can seat 530 people.

"I want my free water," someone is muttering behind me as we drift into the massive store, as if water isn't free almost everywhere these days.

The clerks don't seem fazed at all when the big group filters into the store. They're friendly and smile and say hello. They must be used to bus tours. Either used to, or sick of. Then again, forty-five people could drop a serious amount of cash on souvenirs, so maybe they're excited, although we'd fill less than one-tenth of the restaurant.

Inside, it is postcard heaven. It's the hugest gift shop I've ever been in. Magnets. Jewelry. Black Hills gold, whatever that is. T-shirts, any kind of shirts, a giant wall of cowboy boots.

But there's also all the practical stuff, like shampoo and Advil. You could completely start your life over here with the contents of this store. You might not be exactly chic, but you could do it.

I stand there and fill my hand with postcards, skimming for new ones I haven't seen before, and grabbing as many as I can, as if this is a timed game show and I need to end up with the most prizes.

"I'm going to buy some sneakers for running," Uncle Jeff announces. "And maybe some cowboy boots."

"I'm buying cowgirl boots," Mom says, following him in her Corn Palace sweatshirt. "Keep track of Zena!" she calls over her shoulder, as if I could, as if Zena is even talking to me.

I wander around, considering mugs, glasses, sunglasses. Then I see the SEND AN EMAIL FROM WALL DRUG! sign. I can hardly move fast enough. I push aside some fellow bus-ees who are clogging the hat and bandanna aisle and rush to the computers. There are two of them, and only one is being used.

I check my email and it feels like months since I've done that, instead of only days. I'm expecting dozens, but since I told everyone I was going to be gone there are only a few random ones. But there's one from Dylan. So nothing else really matters.

AREIL,
Just in case you get email after all, 'cause it turns out we do this year. Got a few of your postcards. Thanks. Sounds like you're having fun.

It does? Really? Because I'm not, I instant-message him, but he's not online, which is probably a good thing, because that sounded weak. Again, I'm the kind of person who needs time to write something good. Rush into things and I come out sounding horrible.

Of course, I don't misspell someone's *name*; for instance I don't write DILLON, or DLYN.

Anyway. Wyoming is very cool, and camp's great, but way too busy. My first day off isn't for another week. I've met lots of people. Half the counselors are new, and I was voted in charge of the sports activities. We have a big competition in two weeks, all the cabins compete.
Areil, don't sweat it if things don't work out this summer. I know I'm gone a long time and we really aren't serious or anything. But you are cute.
CU, Dylan

My heart is pounding. I immediately start to type:

DYLAN, YOU WON'T BELIEVE THIS—WE ARE ALMOST IN WYOMING TOO!

And I sense someone looming over my shoulder and prepare my defense for Mom, but it won't be too hard because I didn't say anything bad about her yet, or anything too risqué, but it isn't Mom. And it isn't Zena, either, for a change.

It's Andre. It makes me feel weird to be writing even more to Dylan in front of him, like that's all I do or something. Which isn't true. Except maybe lately it is.

"Hey," he says. "You might want to turn off the caps lock."

"Not like you're reading over my shoulder *again*, or anything," I complain.

"Sorry. Just caught my eye." He slides into the now-empty seat at the counter next to me.

"Just caught your eye," I mutter. "Yeah. Right."

"It did! I'm sorry," he says, laughing as I turn my back toward him and resume attempting to write in all caps.

"Five minutes to a customer, okay?" The clerk behind the counter smiles and sets the electronic timer on top of each computer.

I start typing like crazy, but I do so much pausing and revising that I actually end up taking forever just to say a couple of things. Beside me, Andre has already written a novel or two, mailed to multiple addresses, created a trip blog, etc. I don't actually know this but I can hear how fast his fingers hit the keys, and it's entirely possible.

I lamely write:

I DON'T KNOW HOW YOU CAN CALL ME, WE'RE TOTALLY PHONELESS, BUT IF YOU SEND EMAILS I WILL TOO AT THE NEXT PLACE WE STOP. I THINK WE ARE GOING TO BE REALLY CLOSE TO YOUR CAMP. I JUST HAVE THIS FEELING.

Why did I use that phrase? Why didn't I think before I decided to tack that on at the last second? I want to hit delete because that sounded idiotic, but it's too late.

"So how's the boyfriend?" Andre asks as the timer rings, sounding like we've just completed a round in a prizefight. We both stand up, and immediately new emailers slide into our vacated seats.

"He's great." I smile, sincerely this time, because I am really happy about the turn of events.

"Where is he again?" Andre asks.

"Wyoming," I say. "It's a small town near Casper." We stand by a large wall of maps, and I point out where Camp Far-a-Way is located. It's not all that close to where we're going—yet—unless of course that *is* where we're going, because you never know with Leisure-Lee Tours.

"Come on, we have to check out the T. rex outside in the backyard."

"We do?" I ask.

"We do. That's what we do, remember? Investigate the backyard sculpture gardens of the Wild West." We stroll along past various displays. "A person could really get lost in here," Andre comments. "I mean, which room were we in?"

"I don't know."

We walk past photos of the Old West, of Wall Drug throughout history. We stop at the gigantic restaurant and I peek inside to see what kind of place can actually seat multiple bus tours, over five hundred people.

I spy Zena and Bethany sitting at the table, and go in to say hi and check on her. "Do you need some money?" I ask.

"No," she says, and then she slurps whatever's in her cup with a straw. "Bethany's treating."

"Because I have money," I insist. "And you could have some of it."

"No, thanks. We're good," says Bethany.

Zena stares over at Andre, who's standing in the doorway, leaning against the host stand. "Hey. I thought you liked Dylan," she says.

I shrug. "I do. I was just emailing him, actually."

"So why are you with *him* all the time?" She gestures toward the doorway.

"Why are you with Bethany all the time?" I counter. "I mean, who else am I supposed to hang out with?"

"But he's *weird*," says Zena. "He says everything in threes."

"You're weird." I grab one of her French fries and head over to Andre.

We're sitting in a photo booth having our picture taken as we pose like Western heroes when suddenly the curtain opens.

"*There* you are," Jenny says. "We've all been looking for you."

"You ruined the shot!" Andre complains. "You totally ruined the shot, and it was going to be the best one." He stands there and waits for the photo strip to print, then shows Jenny the last one, where we're both looking sideways and it's no good. He's right.

But Jenny's too wound up to care. "I just looked up an events schedule for the time we're around Mount Rushmore. There isn't a 10K like you thought."

"Oh." I feel the excitement sink out of me like a deflated balloon, without the embarrassing *pffft* sound, thank goodness. It's hard to ignore the fact that Jenny seems elated by this news, as if it's her life's mission to disappoint me.

"But there *is* a marathon." Jenny smiles so widely that I can see she is the type who flosses and whitens her teeth daily.

"Oh?" I squeak. A marathon. I've never run that far at one time. I might have run that far in one week.

"Isn't that great?" Jenny hands me a flyer about it and I see it's called the Keystone Key to the Black Hills Marathon, and there's also a fun run and various other activities, so I should be able to handle something. "You can enter the marathon," she says. "Isn't that great?"

What am I going to do, say no? "It's *so* great," I say, that is, if you consider major muscle damage and emergency ambulance rides to hospitals in strange towns great.

That gives me seven days to get in shape. Seven days to contact Dylan and see if he can meet me. And when he does meet me, I'll be absolutely exhausted.

But who cares?

"And we'll all be there to cheer you on," Jenny says. "There are so many of us that we can easily spread out on the course, so you'll never be too far from someone rooting for you."

"Because that's the way we run marathons," Andre says in an unnatural, syrupy voice. "Leisure-Lee style!"

Jenny glares at him. "Anyway, you two, it's time to go. Come on, everyone's waiting outside. We're all ready."

"I'm going to buy a soda first," Andre announces. "I'll grab one for you."

"Jenny, we just got here," I say. "We've been reading about this place forever and—"

"I know, but we got off schedule."

"Schedule?" I narrow my eyes at her. "I thought we didn't have a schedule."

"Don't be difficult. We need a place to sleep tonight, and we don't want a repeat of last night, driving around, calling for reservations. Come on, get your things and let's giddyap."

"I have my things. I don't even have . . . things that I take off the bus," I say. She looks at me as if I've just given her too much information, and I probably have. "But I just have one question. What about Wyoming?"

Jenny folds her arms in front of her and looks at me. "What about it?"

"Are we going there, too?" I ask.

"Interesting question. You should know by now that you never know with Leisure-Lee. Just enjoy the journey, Zena." She turns and walks away in a sort of huff.

"Ariel!" I call after her. "A-R-I-E-L!"

So I go out to the bus, but then I claim to need something personal from the pharmacy department, and so I'm off the bus again and sprinting into Wall Drug and there's a family using both computers, but I beg them to let me send just one short email, and they do.

Dylan
We will be near Mount Rushmore on June 21.
It's a Saturday.
Be there!

I quickly buy a few small bags of Skittles and dash outside. My uncle is rushing to the bus ahead of me. He has boxes balanced precariously in front of him as he speed-walks to the bus: boxes of cowboy boots, moccasins, sandals, and every other kind of shoe, it seems, but sneakers.

He can't see where he's going, of course, and when he trips on a small rock in the road, the boxes start to topple, then crash to the ground. I run to help him, catching what I can in midair and crouching down to the ground to help reassemble the rest.

Uncle Jeff shakes his head. "I'm so clumsy. I'm a complete klutz."

I stare at him, and there's a sadness on his face I've never seen before. "No, you're not," I say.

"I'm useless." He sighs. "Absolutely useless."

"You're not," I tell him. "You're the one who keeps us all sane."

He struggles to stack the boxes in his arms again. "Why did I just buy all these things, anyway? I don't even have my full income right now."

"Cheer up, Uncle Jeff," I say as we walk to the bus together, side by side.

That's definitely a sentence I never thought I'd write, let alone say. But I'm in a great mood because we're heading west again, and I'll see Dylan soon. This might be one of my last days on the bus, so why not try to have fun?

"Ariel, you are a niece and a half," Uncle Jeff says.

I smile, not sure what that means. "Thanks. I think."

Wall, South Dakota: a traveler's—and shopper's—dream come true.

D—

We just went to Wall Drug. It's HUGE. AWESOME. Everything the billboards say. Seriously.
   The no-cent ice water and 5-cent coffee were both excellent.
   Anyway, as you can see, still heading west. Next stop: Badlands.
   See you soon. I hope I hope.
   Love,
   A

I...lI..lI..lI.t.lIII...dI...iII...lI..l.I.t.lIIt.lI.t.....I.lI

Chapter Thirteen

I barely have time to finish the postcard because The Badlands turn out to be only, like, ten miles away, and our motel is only fifteen. I could probably run back to Wall and email Dylan again—and pick up some more snacks—but apparently I won't need to, because this is the kind of travel stop that offers it all, which is nice because we're going to be here for a few days. Huge motel, huge lounge, huge restaurant, huge pool. But it's sort of dated, so they have everything except huge Internet access, which seems very bizarre, but there's some claim to be letting us experience history.

It's weird because the whole landscape is suddenly getting larger; everything's getting bigger—the sky, the land, and now even the motels.

It sort of feels, and looks, like we're on the moon. The mountains look like giant sand hills, but with a purplish tint. I've never seen anything like them before. They're sort of the color of the Grand

Canyon, but not exactly. They look like a giant made a series of sand castles, the kind where you pour water over sand until they clump into drips and shapes.

After a quick driving tour of Badlands National Park, we check into our motel and everyone stops to stare through the fence at the giant pool, clinging to the chain-link as if we're jailed and looking at freedom on the other side.

Before I hit the pool I go running with my grandfather, and with Uncle Jeff trailing us, speed-walking, wearing his new cross-training sandals. They're actually a cross between flip-flops and sneakers and look really uncomfortable. He keeps talking about the shock-absorbing soles, which must be something if they can absorb the shock of Uncle Jeff trying to run in them.

I shouldn't be so catty. He is really making an effort to be out here with me, and that does count for a lot, but I'm secretly worried he'll be in the background of my photo for the cover of *Runners World* someday. *She used to train with her uncle, who was a master of shoe trickery,* the magazine article will say. *It took years for her to recover from the thirteen-minute-mile pace and regain her strength, and by that time she was thirty. She missed qualifying at the Olympic Trials three times in a row. She was considered a never-been.*

"Ariel, you're really picking up the pace," my grandfather comments.

I must have been thinking too hard. "I have to pick up the pace," I tell him. "There's a marathon I have to run a week from Saturday."

"What? We can't do a marathon," he says. "That would be foolish. We haven't been training nearly enough."

"I know. Maybe there's a half marathon, though."

"Oh. All right, fine. That we could pull off."

"Seriously?" I ask.

"Sure. We could run that tonight," Grandpa says. "Well, except for not being able to see very well. When is it again?"

"The twenty-first. Jenny told me about it. It's outside Rapid City, I think a town called Keystone, and I'm not sure what altitude that is—"

I haven't even finished talking when it's as if little rockets appear on the backs of my grandfather's shoes and he's off, sprinting. We run intervals; then we time each other doing miles; then Uncle Jeff times us. We're a team in training. We can't be stopped. At the end of it, I'm out of breath, my uncle has a sunburned nose, and my grandfather has hardly broken a sweat.

"What are you made out of, exactly?" I ask him.

"Pardon?"

"You're like a man of steel. You have zero body fat. You never get tired," I comment.

"Experience, kid. And you don't have much on you, either." He squeezes my bicep. "Probably it's from being the head of this family. It makes you tough."

"Really?"

He looks to the sky and sighs. "You have no idea."

When we get back I change into my bikini and head out to the pool, which is mobbed, like no one has ever seen water before. My grandmother is sitting by the pool, giving Zena a pedicure while Zena "reads" the latest issue of *InStyle*. Mom is reading the new Dr. Phil book, because that's what she does for fun, keeps up on her "contemporaries," as she calls them. Sometimes I wish Dr. Phil would show up at her office and listen to her life story and ask, "And how's that working for you?"

Andre is sitting there in a T-shirt that says REALITY BITES, wearing long shorts and flip-flops. He's bopping his head to his iPod, the vocabulary book open on his lap to the Ks.

"Why aren't you in the pool?" I ask.

"Why isn't anybody? The water's chilled. Cold. Frigid," Andre says.

"But the air is extremely hot. Burning. Suffocating. Swim already," I tell him.

"Yeah, maybe." When he takes off his T-shirt and stretches his arms over his head, I can't help looking at his body. He has those cut muscles in his stomach, the ones runners and other athletes get when they're incredibly lean. I wonder how he gets them, because he doesn't run endlessly like me, and he seems not to care about being an athlete, though I guess I don't have much proof of anything. All I know is that I should probably stop looking at him and his cut body.

I sit on the pool's edge and stick my feet into the water. "Okay, so it's not warm." When I turn to look at him over my shoulder, I see him kind of staring at me. He coughs, embarrassed, and so I slide into the pool, even though it's cold enough to make me gulp.

"Come on, get in," I urge him.

He slides off his flip-flops and sits on the edge, near me, his feet in the water.

"You call that in?" I ask.

He flicks water in my face with his foot. "Give me a second."

I tug at his foot, and he gives up and jumps in. "Man. You think it'd be warmer," he says.

"You'd think," I agree.

We swim around for a while to warm up, then attempt to float, which is difficult now that people like my grandpa are swimming laps. We swim over to the edge and hold on, treading water in the deep end. It feels comfortable being with him, but sort of exciting, too. I'm not sure what's going on with him—or us.

Mom comes over to the edge near us and sits down. "So, Andre. Tell me about yourself," she says.

I look at her, my eyes narrowed. If she doesn't get into the pool soon, I will push her in. And possibly hold her down for a second or two, just to scare her.

"What would you like to know?" he asks, a lot more politely than I probably would.

"Well, what do you do for fun? Are you on any teams, in any clubs, do you read, do you only eat Skittles . . . ?"

"Don't give him the third degree, Mom," I warn.

"I play lacrosse," he says. "I have my library card, which is well-worn. And I vote. No, wait, I don't, because I'm only sixteen."

"So you'll be a junior in the fall, like Ariel?"

"A senior."

"How did you manage that?"

Andre pulls himself out of the water and heads for his towel. "I skipped a grade."

"That's impressive. I'm always telling Ariel to take AP classes as soon as she can. They're *such* an advantage."

I submerge and swim down to the bottom of the pool, staying there until I run out of breath. Then I get out, dry myself off a little, and flop onto a chair, facedown, my back to the sky. The sun starts to bake the water off my back. I love that feeling. This finally feels like vacation.

"See, if we went on a cruise, Mother, this would be our day. This would be so awesome," Zena is saying to Mom, who has finally stopped quizzing Andre.

"Boring," Mom says, pushing up her organic cotton sleeves. She refuses to take off her shirt, even though she has a bathing suit on underneath, and even though she made me look at the Lands' End site with her for about thirty-six hours picking out said swimsuit. "Pools are boring. And cruises are environmentally unsound."

Uncle Jeff does a cannonball off the diving board, completely splashing everyone.

Andre comes over to sit beside me in a webbed chair, and I turn to him. "That's my positive male influence. Him."

Andre unfolds the chair so he can lie down beside me, and it collapses with a crash, nearly tossing him onto the concrete deck. "Figures," he says. He unfolds it again and slides into it carefully. "Ariel, look."

I feel a tap on my shoulder and I turn over.

Andre gestures to Lenny, who's fast asleep in a lounge chair. Then he points to Jenny, who's busy playing water volleyball with some of the seniors. "This would be the perfect time to figure out our route. Or just find out some dirt about Lenny and Jenny. Or hide all the old people's travel pillows and watch them freak out when they get on the bus tomorrow."

I smile, picturing the chaotic scene. "Okay, but how are we going to get on it?"

"Come on," Andre urges. "Maybe we will, maybe we won't. But if we stay here, your mom's going to grill me some more."

I'm up for any nonfamily adventure, so I slide on my flip-flops, wrap a towel around me, and together we head out of the pool area. Why am I tiptoeing? I wonder.

"Ariel? Andre! Where are you going?" Mom calls to me.

Maybe that's why. "Just getting something to drink. We'll be right back," I say. "It figures that she sensed I was leaving. She's got Ariel radar," I comment to Andre.

"Don't take long!" she calls after us. "And bring me a coffee, okay?"

"I want an iced tea!" Mrs. O'Neill adds. "And not the green kind. And put some sugar in it!"

"How is this different from being at home, again?" Andre asks as we open the gate and head out to the parking lot. "Wait. Hold on." He grabs my arm midway to the bus. "The door's open. Why is the door open?"

"I don't know," I say. "Someone's cleaning it?"

"This is it. This is our chance. Maybe they left the keys, too," he says.

I find that I'm still tiptoeing, which isn't a good thing, because as I take my first step up onto the bus, I trip on my towel and nearly wipe out.

I grab Andre, who's ahead of me, to keep from doing a face-plant onto the steering wheel.

"Coordinated much?" he jokes, turning around to help me catch my balance. His hand's on my waist, and that's when I realize that my towel is now lying on the steps behind me. I'm not naked, but it's as close as I've ever been, standing this near to a guy.

"No, seriously. You're in really good shape. Really good," he says. "I'm sorry I made that crack about runners back in whatever town that was."

"It's okay. I mean, thanks." I feel this weird tension between us.

"Obviously it's something you take seriously and all, so . . ."

"Right."

"So."

"So."

Pool water drips off my hair and slides down the middle of my back, which is good because I'm getting seriously hot in here. I feel like

Andre is about to kiss me, or maybe it's that I'm about to kiss him.

"Excuse me. Where are we?" Andre and I jump back from each other as a sleepy-looking old woman approaches us down the aisle. I'm pretty sure it's Ethel.

"Um . . . at the motel pool?" I say, unable to think of the name of the motel, still in shock over the fact that I almost made a move on Andre, which is ridiculous, because isn't going west and sneaking onto buses all about seeing Dylan?

"I must have been asleep when we got here, so they just let me be. Ha!" Ethel chuckles. "How funny. Haven't been able to sleep a wink since this trip started—blasted roommate snores like a freight train. So, what have I missed?"

"Honestly? Not too much," Andre tells her.

"Right." I struggle to retrieve my towel before Andre helps her down the steps. As we walk back into the pool area, I realize that I completely forgot my mom's coffee. Fortunately, we have Ethel to cover for us.

Big Badlands Motor Court—too big to fit on a small postcard! All-inclusive resort. Try our famous chuck-wagon supper, sip cocktails in the Pronghorn Lounge, or hit the pool with the kids! AARP discount rates.

Sarah,
This bus can apparently time travel. Check out the place on the front. We're back in the sixties. Or seventies. Turn on the History Channel and maybe you'll see us.
    Temperature is in the high eighties. "But it's a dry heat," all the older people on the bus keep saying.
    Help me, I'm writing about the weather. This place has a fantabulous pool.
    Have tons to tell you.
    XO
    Me

Chapter Fourteen

The next night, after hiking all day and being at a chuck-wagon supper for most of the night, we go to our motel room and Mom slides every single bar and lock on our door closed. As if Zena and I were both thinking of slipping out sometime during the night. And as if we couldn't unbolt all of the locks without waking her up, because she's a very sound sleeper.

I look over at Zena as I'm brushing my teeth. Is she thinking what I'm thinking—about escaping? But she's busy reading a fresh copy of *Entertainment Weekly* that she stole from the lobby earlier.

I go lie down beside her on the bed, which is fortunately a queen this time and big enough for both of us. I think about when we were little and Zena went through this stage on one trip when she couldn't sleep, and the four of us would crowd into one bed and all roll up together.

"So, Zena," I say, looking at her as I prop up on one elbow. "What's been your favorite part so far?"

"Hanging out with Bethany and the guys."

"The guys?"

"Dieter and Wolfgang," she says. "Who else?"

"But what *else*?" asks Mom. "You two cannot make this entire trip about boys. I forbid you."

Zena rolls her eyes at Mom and puts a pillow under her neck. "The antelopes, then." She tosses another pillow into the air and catches it with her feet.

"You're kidding," I say. "I didn't see them. You want to tell me about it?"

"Not really," she says.

"You would have noticed them too, Ariel, if you weren't spending so much time working on your postcards and hanging out with Andre," Mom says.

I ignore her postcard comment, because if she can't appreciate that I want to write them, then I can't explain it to her. "It's impossible not to spend so much time with anyone on the bus when you're *on a bus*. Captive audience and all," I point out.

"Yes, but this is a family trip," she says. "It's about the family. Spend time visiting with your grandparents, your uncle. In fact, starting tomorrow, you'll be sitting with one of us."

"Since when are you in charge of seating assignments?" I ask. "Did Jenny appoint you?"

"Ariel, don't take that tone with me. I'm in charge. Period."

"Oh, really. Were you in charge when Dad was taking our money and—"

"Why are you bringing this up now?"

I throw up my hands. "Why not?"

"We've gone over this. Your father always handled the bills, the banking, balancing the checking account, all of that. We never had a problem before, and there was no reason to suspect anything." She brushes and rebrushes her unruly hair.

I think about it. I know what she's saying is mostly true. It's only when I look back that I can see all the omens, or warning signs, and maybe it's the same for her.

"Anyway, back to tomorrow. You'll sit with family. Both of you should get to know your uncle and grandparents better. I mean, what if we end up living closer to them? Wouldn't that be nice?"

I feel like a trapdoor in the floor just opened and I'm about to fall into it. What is she talking about? "You want to move all the way to St. Paul? No," I say. "No, you can move, but I'm not."

"I didn't say we *would*; I just said that it would be nice."

Zena lifts her head from her pillow long enough to say, "That sounds sort of cool."

I glare at her closed eyes. I can't believe she's siding with Mom, even if she's half-asleep.

"Ariel? Forget your knee-jerk reaction and think about it. How would you really feel about that?" Mom asks.

"You know what? I don't want to talk about it. I want to stay where I am. It's junior year for me, Mom. It's not the time to just . . . start over."

"But can't you understand . . . maybe getting a fresh start would be a good idea for all of us?"

"Fresh start. That's like a breakfast cereal, right?" I turn off my light and snuggle under the covers, letting her know I am done for the night with this conversation.

"Ariel, Ariel, come on, let's talk," Mom urges as she slides into the other bed. "Nothing's ever solved by not talking."

"Maybe this will be the first time. Good night," I say.

I desperately want to fall asleep and forget this conversation, but

I don't drift off into dreamland the way I'd like to. Zena falls asleep, and then Mom falls asleep, while I lie there and think. I wait until my mother is snoring, then get up.

"I can't sit with you on the bus tomorrow."

Andre sits down across from me in the lobby. He's wearing shorts and a rumpled Marquette University T-shirt. "Is that why you called and woke me up? To tell me that?"

"No," I say, feeling kind of miserable. "Well, yeah."

"Okay." Andre rubs his eyes underneath his glasses. "Why can't you sit with me? Is it because your grandfather hates me?"

"What? No." I shake my head. "Why would he hate you?"

"Because I'm black?"

"Oh, really? You are? Huh."

"Shut up."

"No, he doesn't hate you, for that or anything else. He's just . . . protective. So if we spend time together, he's just . . . he wants to know you better. I guess. Anyway, my mom went on and on about how it's a family trip and I'm supposed to sit with my family. And now my mom is talking about us moving to Minnesota."

Andre yawns. "So what do you want to do? Should we sneak on the bus again?"

"I can't believe we'd want to spend *more* time there. I feel like that seat fabric pattern is becoming one with my skin. Everywhere I look, I see mauve diamonds."

"Stand up and let me see if it's coming off on you," Andre orders, nudging my leg with his foot.

"Shut up." I look over and see the desk clerk staring at us. "Come on, let's go outside."

* * *

We go out by the pool, which is open until midnight, although there isn't anyone actually in it. We pull two chairs close to each other and lie down.

Andre looks up at the stars and takes a deep breath. "This place is kind of awesome," he says. "I mean, it's *way* out here. I've never seen so many stars."

I gaze upward, too, looking for some kind of constellation I can point out, but I don't see anything. "Kind of awesome? That doesn't sound like you. Give me three words."

"Trance-inducing. Relaxing. Cool." He sighs. "I'm really tired. My vocabulary is lame right now. Lame as in pathetic, useless." He looks over at me. "So what's the deal with moving and not sitting together?"

I groan. "Thanks for reminding me," I say, but it's not as though I've had time to forget.

"Sorry. But what's going on?" he asks.

"It's . . . She wants me to get to know her side of the family better, because she's sick of my dad's, I guess, or just my dad. So she wants us to maybe move all the way to St. Paul to get away from him."

"Bad divorce?" Andre asks, adjusting the chair another notch so that he lies almost flat.

"You could say that. My dad . . . well, he kept going to work every morning, but it turned out he didn't actually have a job anymore; he was going to the racetrack. And the casino. Which is where he spent all our college money. After he ran through all the money he embezzled from his work. He didn't tell us any of this. We found out when he was arrested, and then it broke on TV, and it was all over school."

I didn't mean to say so much, but once I started I somehow couldn't stop. So there it is, out in the open. Like a bag lunch on a picnic table waiting for someone to pick it up or toss it. Or trade it for turkey.

"That's like . . . the longest sentence I've ever heard you say," Andre says.

"This stupid trip. It's getting to me," I mutter.

"Road rage?"

"Something like that. My mom's a counselor and she published some self-help books, but she's kind of clueless about people. She sits in her office listening to people pour out their relationship troubles, while her own marriage is going up in flames. And scratch cards. And horses." I pause. "Well, not that the horses are going up in flames; that sounds disgusting."

Andre laughs. "So. Are you and your dad still in touch?"

"Oh yeah. I'm just . . . Honestly? I'm still really blown away by what happened. He started acting really hyper and fidgety. Then he was never home. Then he was arrested. It's like . . . all these little funny traits he had were exaggerated and they weren't funny anymore. Like, we used to bet about things all the time, but I thought it was just a game to him. I guess whenever I'm around him, I feel nervous. Because I don't know who he is. He's a wild card. If he could do that to us once—over the course of, like, years—and he only stopped six months ago, when he *had* to . . ."

"Well, is he twelve-stepping it?" asks Andre.

I smile and nod in admiration. "That's a good one," I say.

"What?"

"Nothing. Zena and I just try to come up with new words and—"

"It's not a new word."

"Never mind." I sigh. "Yeah, he's making amends. Or claiming to."

"Hey, it's just your dad. You know?" Andre reaches over and puts his hand on my wrist, giving it a little squeeze. "It's not you."

"Right." It doesn't seem to matter that I know this, though. "So. What about you?" I ask, tired of telling and hearing my story.

"Everything seems pretty good for you. So why do you want to run away?"

"I'm sick of being good. Good is overrated," he says with a sigh.

"You tried to break into a tour bus. You call that being good?" I laugh.

"Living with my mom . . . She won't let me visit my dad. She thinks he's a bad influence, which he really isn't, and anyway, I'm old enough to decide things on my own. If I think he's a jerk, I'll be okay. Right?"

"When did they get divorced?"

"When I was six."

"Why?"

"Who knows?"

"You don't?"

"A hundred reasons, I guess. No, wait. A hundred other women, I think it was. Yeah. Anyway, I wanted to spend the summer with him in L.A. He wanted me to. Mom said no. She had no really good reason, and she's always urging us to get closer—but spend more than holidays together? No. Not an option."

I wonder about my future and how things like that will shake out. Will I see Dad on Thanksgiving or Christmas? Who will decide? Is Mom even allowed to take us that far away?

"Then she comes up with this trip idea. You don't know how many times we argued about this. 'We'll bond, Andre,' she said. 'No, *you'll* have a good time; I'll be bored to death,' I said. I mean, if you weren't here?" He pretends to hold a gun to his head.

"No way. You'd hang out with Ethel."

"Yeah. Dentures are *so* sexy."

"So that's why you'd head to L.A. if you could. You and Ethel, I mean," I say.

"I'm thinking about it," he replies. "Well, not the Ethel part."

"I'm thinking about meeting up with Dylan," I tell him. Like, that's pretty much all I think about—or did, until my encounter with Andre on the bus.

"You are? For real?"

"Sure. What's stopping me?" I ask.

"Well, um, a car. A bus. A bunch of relatives. A *plan*."

Not that he has a negative outlook or anything. "I have a plan," I say. I think it over. "Not a good plan. But, uh, Dylan could meet me and then I'd leave with him."

"And he's working at this camp. So what would you do? Go back there with him and get hired on, too? Or be a really old camper?"

"No, of course not. We'd travel together," I say.

"With no car," Andre says. "And like, how much money?"

I glare at him. I don't want to stay here. Or move to Dylan's camp. Or follow through on any of my options.

"My plan's better," Andre says confidently. "We somehow get to Denver. Whether it's on this bus or another bus."

"Okay. Then what?"

Suddenly a flashlight beam bounces across the deck, coming to rest on my face. "Excuse me, but the pool is closed," a man's voice announces.

"Grandpa?" I ask, shielding my eyes from the flashlight. "What are those, extra-strength batteries?"

He walks over to us and looks down at the way we're nearly sprawled on the concrete in our flat lounge chairs. "It's past your bedtime, isn't it?"

"We're too old to have bedtimes," I say.

"Hm. So am I," Grandpa says, "and yet I have one." He looks up at the sky and lets out a deep sigh. "On the other hand, it's nice out here. Our A/C unit is broken and the breeze has yet to find its way into our room."

He drags a chair over next to mine. Then he pulls his Nike headband out of his pocket. "Give me your hand," he says.

I don't know what's going on, but I do it, and Grandpa wraps the headband around both of our wrists, locking them together.

"You're cuffing me," I say.

"Call it what you like. This way if I'm asleep and you try to leave, I'll know about it."

"Do you want *me* to leave?" asks Andre.

"I don't care one way or the other, but if you do leave, don't take her with you."

"Yes, sir," Andre says, sounding intimidated.

Grandpa leans back in his chair next to mine, our arms propped on the armrest together. "Now. Don't let me interrupt. What were you two plotting just now when I walked in?" he asks.

"What else?" I say. "How to steal the *Oklahoma!* CD."

"I'm in," says Grandpa, and we all lie back, look up at the stars, and contemplate ways to get to Lenny and Jenny.

Dylan,
Have you ever been to the Badlands?
    They are a lot more interesting than I thought.
    Except that we had to attend a chuck-wagon supper, where they served buffalo burgers, baked beans, and blond brownies. And other things beginning with B, like beer.
    I stuck to Skittles. Or actually, it was so hot out that the Skittles stuck to me.
    Hope you're having a good time.
    XO
    A

I...II...II.,.II.,l.III...dl...,II...II...I.I.,I.II.I.,I.t......I.II

Chapter Fifteen

The next morning, I nearly lose my breakfast when the bus goes roaring past the turnoff for Rapid City.

A detour? Again?

I don't just feel ill because I really wanted to go there, but also because Jenny takes this curve kind of too fast while I'm looking down at a postcard, and the fried-egg sandwich at the hot breakfast buffet seems like it wasn't such a great idea after all. Which is what I thought, but Grandma kept insisting I eat more, especially if I was planning on running as much as I have been, and Grandpa and I had just come back from a nine-mile run. (He covered for me not being in my room in the morning, saying I went to their room early that morning for a visit, which made my mother smile, and my grandmother look confused.) "Wasting away" is what she called it. "It's time for you to carb up," she kept saying, as if "carb" were a verb, as she carried over more wheat toast from the burn-it-yourself toaster. So I caved and carbed, and now the carbs are coming back up.

"But I thought . . . Excuse me, aren't we going to Rushmore?" I call up toward the front of the bus.

My voice is just one of the dozens asking the same question.

Lenny stands and faces us. "Yes, but if there's one thing I've learned over the years, it's this: You can't rush Mount Rushmore." He makes that annoying clicking noise with his tongue, and Jenny revs the engine, and I wonder if the two actions are connected, like she's ticked at him. I wonder how many times each summer they do this tour, how often she's had to listen to his presentations, how many times he's had to help her fix the bus.

"You can't?" someone asks.

"Nope. You cannot rush Mount Rushmore. You've got to anticipate. You've got to wait. Then you've absolutely got to see it from the right angle, from the right road. We'll see some other interesting sites first, and then we'll do a loop around and end up approaching from another direction, with breathtaking views. Rushmore is something you approach slowly, deliberately."

It sounds like a speech Lenny has crafted over the years, but that doesn't make it any less annoying.

"Well, I guess we just have to take his word for it," Uncle Jeff says to me.

We're sitting next to each other, as ordered by my mother. I don't even know if Uncle Jeff is happy about it. He's made lots of friends on the trip—maybe he'd rather sit with one of them.

"Guess so," I say.

"You know what, Ariel? All this running we've been doing over the past week?" He nods his head, and so do I. "It's really helping me. Every morning when I wake up I feel like my muscles are really alive."

"So you're getting over the, um, injury and stuff?" I ask.

He nods again. "I think so. I mean, it could be a while yet. But I feel stronger. I feel like I could conquer the world."

"That's cool," I comment. "I'm glad. But is it really the running?"

"You tell me," he says.

"Tell you what?" I ask.

"Is it the running?" he says. "Is that why you run so far, so often?"

"Sure. I guess."

"Because it makes sense I'd like it, genetically— Wait a second, hold on. There's Sturgis. Sturgis! I haven't been there in years. Why aren't we stopping? Lenny!" he calls. "Why aren't we getting off here?"

"Because this isn't one of our stops," Lenny replies.

"We're not stopping in Sturgis?" Uncle Jeff sounds stunned. "But we're going right through it."

"Exactamundo!" Lenny makes that clicking noise with his tongue. "We're going right past without stopping."

"But if you can't rush, uh, Mount Rushmore, then you can't, uh, leave Sturgis in the lurch-is," Uncle Jeff says.

"Work on it, mate, and get back to me," Lenny says, sounding like Simon Cowell on *American Idol*.

Uncle Jeff slumps in his seat, looking sort of like a kid who was just told he wasn't getting his favorite toy for Christmas. I feel bad for him. This crazy bus trip might not have been *his* idea, either. "Do you want to ask for a bus vote?" I suggest. "Other people might want to see Sturgis."

His eyebrows shoot up, like that hadn't occurred to him. But then he shrugs and slumps down again. "I don't know, Ariel. Why tempt fate? Maybe it's a sign."

I look out the window, confused. "What's a sign?"

"My life. My Harley days. My motorcycle rally days. They're over," he says. "I have to move on."

"Just like that?"

"If I was still that person . . . well, I wouldn't be here on a bus, would I? I'd be meeting you in Sturgis because I rode there on my motorcycle." He taps the armrest between us. "I've changed; my methods of perambulation have changed."

I poke my head up over the seat back, where Andre's sitting with his mom and Cuddles behind us. Mrs. O'Neill has suddenly gotten interested in this "sitting with family" concept, too. She and Mom are conspiring, no doubt. "Perambulation?" I ask Andre.

"Technically it means tour of duty, but he probably means getting around," Andre replies instantly. Then he asks, "Your uncle gets around?"

"Not like that. On a motorcycle," I explain.

"Well, dudes on motorcycles sometimes *do* get around, you know."

"Shut up," I whisper. "You're talking about my uncle." I smile, then sit back down, while Uncle Jeff is explaining that Sturgis has a gigantic motorcycle rally every August, and how he used to go, how that was always his summer vacation week, how he'd arrange it far in advance, and how he met so many fellow carriers and even had a romance there once with a postal inspector named Sandra.

I look out the window at the signs, trying to miss some of the intimate details he's sharing. We're heading toward a town called Deadwood, which sounds familiar for some reason.

I feel a pen press on my ribs, and reach between the seats to grab it. Andre and I wrestle for it until a shadow looms over me.

"I'll be confiscating that highlighter now," Mrs. O'Neill says.

"That's the first thing they take away in jail. The pens," Andre comments.

* * *

As everyone gets off the bus in Deadwood, I sit and wait until I'm the last one. "We are still *going* to Mount Rushmore, right?" I ask Jenny, who's sitting in the driver's seat. "Even though we're not rushing it."

She laughs. "Yes, of course we're going there."

"And I can still run that race on the twenty-first. The one in Keystone," I say, hoping to jog her memory, so to speak.

"Possibly, yes," says Jenny.

"Possibly?" I want to scream, but I hold it inside.

"I don't see why not, but on the other hand, you never know. The trip is ten days, and how we spend those ten days . . . well, it's not all set in stone." She shrugs and adjusts something in the little compartment above her seat.

"You know what? I don't know how you guys stay in business. This is the most wishy-washy trip I've ever been on in my entire life."

"Wishy-washy? What are you, twelve?" She snorts.

I glare at her. "No, that's my sister, Zena. The one whose name you keep calling me? My name is Ariel, okay?"

"Are you interested in achieving personal growth or not? Just relax," she says to me.

And what are you, my mother? I want to say. "Relax? How can I relax when I don't know where we're going? When one day you tell me I can do this race, and three days later suddenly you're not sure. Can I or can't I?" I demand.

"We'll see!" Jenny responds with a phony smile. "Now move along; I have to go park the bus."

When I stomp off the bus, my family is waiting at the bottom of the steps, looking concerned by my behavior.

"How can you get so riled up about running? God. It's just *running*," says Zena.

"Thanks for the support, as always," I tell her.

Fortunately, Grandma falls into step beside me. "Jenny's not exactly known for her people skills, is she?"

The first place we head to is Saloon No. 10, and Lenny tells us that this is where the famous Wild Bill Hickok, criminal at large in the 1800s, was killed in 1876. He was shot in the back of the head while playing cards. He had what is now known as the "dead man's hand," a pair of aces and a pair of eights. No news on the fifth card, but apparently also a dead man's card.

There are actors in historical costumes dressed up and walking around the streets, and it turns out we're only a day early for the town's Wild Bill Hickok Days, which is kind of annoying, because I bet those would be pretty fun.

I can't believe I wrote that sentence, either. But I'm serious.

We're also too early for the reenactment of the shooting, which happens every day at three p.m., which is okay because I don't like to think of poker players getting shot in the back of the head. Wild Bill's "dead man's chair," or a replica of it, hangs from the wall.

I start to get that nauseated feeling again. I try to hide it, but it really grips my gut like the way I can feel sick before a race.

Mom isn't doing much better. She's gone a bit pale. She's standing in the doorway, not committing to coming in, just staring at the chair plastered to the wall above the door, as if she's thinking of the title for her next self-help book: *Deadwood Dad, Deadbeat Dad*.

Come to think of it, I haven't asked her in a while if she's working on a new book, and if so, what it's about, but I have a feeling I'm on the right track with this. The Flackjack Track, that is.

Lenny goes over to her, looking concerned, and asks, "You feeling all right, mate?"

"Not exactly," she says.

"Why don't you come over here and sit down?" He tries to guide her to a seat at the bar.

"No—no, thanks," she says.

I watch her for a second, wondering if she's feeling the way I do. Dad isn't here, but yet he is. People are slumped at slots or bouncing on toes at card tables. He worked his way up—or down, depending how you look at it—and was proud of it, like he was really achieving something. Starting at nickel slots. Then quarters. Then dollars.

Then all the dollars.

He told me all about it the first time he apologized, trying to make amends when he started going to Gamblers Anonymous meetings. How once you got the adrenaline rush you couldn't stop. How every time you had the potential to win big, really big, and sometimes you did and it was exhilarating and you couldn't forget how on top of the world you felt, so you were always chasing that feeling again.

Then he told me how he started doing whatever he could to improve his luck, how one time he carried one of my cross-country race medals in his pocket and he won, so he kept carrying it. Which was sweet, I suppose, but also made my medal seem like a carnival token. If I ever win a real medal—gold or silver or bronze—he'd probably steal it and melt it down, or else just pawn it.

In some ways I'd like to cash in a couple dollars and go try my luck at the slots right now, but Mom has this piercingly sad look on her face, and I just can't walk away and ignore that, as much as I want to.

"Hey," I say, going over to her.

She sighs. "Hey."

"Are you thinking what I'm thinking?"

"I don't know." She frowns, more so than before. "That your father would love it here?"

"No. I was thinking we should go get ice cream," I say, trying to change the subject, because how many times can you beat a dead horse?

"Maybe we should. Or maybe we should stand here and try to understand." She gets this very serious look on her face, like she's channeling the ghost of Wild Bill Hickok, and it hurts her to do so.

"Or there's a realsimple solution," I offer. "We could just leave."

As I look around, not wanting to abandon Mom, but not really wanting to hug it out or hang out and talk either, I see a banner in the back of the room that says: SEND AN EMAIL FROM DEADWOOD! FROM WILD BILL HICKOK!

"Excuse me, Mom. Gotta go," I tell her. Family's one thing, but Dylan's another.

I start to type:

Dylan, we're in Deadwood, which is reallyreallyclose to Wyoming. I saw Devils Tower on the map and we're really close but probably not going. Any way you can get a day pass??? Or whatever they call it? After this we're going to Rushmore. Meet me online at 9 tomorrow night and we can IM.

Mom is behind me. "Come on, Ariel, we're leaving, I'm sorry." She tries to take my arm as if I'm six, and she pulls me over to where Lenny is leading the charge, chanting, "Lemon, lemon . . . cherry! Ah, mate, try it again!"

"Lenny, what were you thinking? This isn't appropriate for the kids," Mom is saying, and just as she does Dieter lets out a whoop because he has gotten three in a row and coins are spitting out of the machine like hail from the sky.

"This is supposed to be fun. Relax, Tammy, relax." Lenny puts his arm around my mother and tries to give her a shoulder rub, and she gives him a warning look, backing off.

"It's Tamara," she says. "Not Tammy."

Jenny, who's been off parking the bus at one of the lots reserved for tour buses, walks in just then and sees Lenny kind of accosting Mom, and she comes over and starts hitting him and accusing him of flirting with Mom. Which is extremely ridiculous, but I don't tell her that because she's been so unpleasant that I kind of enjoy watching her squirm with jealousy.

Lenny and Jenny start yelling at each other, and Mom's trying to counsel them about their marriage, and we've suddenly turned into the white-trash Jerry Springer bus tour.

Later in the afternoon, Andre and I skip the day's strange museum of choice in favor of people watching, and for some reason this is okay with our mothers. We have Cuddles with us, which is our excuse. We pick up a couple of coffees and park on a bench on historic Main Street.

Andre holds up Cuddles, checking out their reflected image in the coffee shop's window. "I'm like a glorified dog walker. I mean, how much does this ruin my image?"

I step back and look at him, at his semi-cut body, with his latest cool T-shirt, his great sneakers, his low-rise jeans, his stylish eyeglasses. Carrying a tiny Chihuahua.

"Are you trying to meet someone?" I ask. " 'Cause if so, here, I'll hold him," I offer.

He pushes my arm away. "No, it's okay."

"No, come on, let me," I insist. "Maybe *I'll* meet someone."

Andre rolls his eyes. "Yeah, lots of middle-aged women. Trust me on this."

"I didn't know so many people would be here," I say. "In Deadwood."

"Why wouldn't they be?"

I shrug, then take a sip of my iced latte.

"I have a question. Does being here make you freak a little?"

"A little," I say. "Yeah. I mean, it looks fun. The thing is that I'd probably like it in the casinos. Or genetically I'd maybe love it."

"You think that kind of thing is inherited?"

I shrug. "I don't know. Does anyone know?"

"Well, are your grandparents gambling addicts?"

"No."

"It could be worse, you know. He could have been a drug addict."

"True, but there's a certain glamour to that," I say. I think about Keith Johnson telling me about his addicted brother, and how it didn't count until you got the call from jail.

"No. Not really. Haven't you ever seen those meth-addict posters? I mean, have you even looked at those *teeth*?" He shudders so violently that Cuddles barks, looking alarmed.

"Gambling's very smoky, and the coins and tokens make your hands stink. My dad used to have this weird lemon-lime smell, like he'd bathed in Sprite, and I couldn't figure it out, and we found out later it was from the little wet cloths they give you to clean your hands after handling all those metal tokens at the casino. But they didn't really work. In the end, it was just like my mom finding lipstick on his collar, only it wasn't another woman. Well, unless you consider Lady Luck a woman, I guess."

"Again with the long sentences," he comments.

"Yeah, well." I take a crumpled bag of Skittles out of my pocket and offer him a handful.

"They're melting," he says as he looks at the clump that fell into his palm. "When you run out of Skittles, that's when we'll know it's time to leave." He reaches for the bag. "Getting close?"

He tries to pull the bag out of my hand, and Skittles clatter on the hot pavement. They start sticking to people's shoe and sandal soles as they walk past and make a sort of gooey tap-dance sound.

How hot is it? Hot enough to fry a Skittle on the sidewalk.

Later that afternoon, Lenny keeps glancing at his watch. He taps his pen against the clipboard. We've all reported to the bus. He's finished taking roll, and there's only one person missing: Jenny.

"Well. I guess we'd better go," he says.

"Do you know how to drive one of these?" asks Grandpa.

"Of course, I've got my commercial driver's license, just like my wife," he says. "We trade off all the time."

"Uh-huh," Mrs. O'Neill says, looking suspicious. "Then why haven't they traded off before now?" she comments to the rest of us.

We're trusting—or desperate, take your pick—so we climb back onto the bus. I sit with Grandpa, because so far I've sat with every family member but him. After a couple of misfires the engine purrs to life, and Lenny very, very slowly maneuvers out of the parking lot.

"So long, Deadwood," Grandpa says.

"So long, Jenny," I add.

"I can't say I'll miss her," Grandpa says to me quietly. "Or her musical selec—"

We look at each other as *Oklahoma!* booms out of the overhead speakers. Apparently Lenny can't drive and monitor volume at the same time.

Wild Bill Hickok says, "They don't call it Deadwood for nothing, now, do they?"

Dear Mars, Incorporated,

You should know that Skittles don't travel all that well.

On hot days, they will melt on sidewalks. Also, the price could be lowered for those of us unable to get summer jobs because our mothers insist on dragging us all over the country.

Thank you for sustaining me and for your great product. My home address is below in case you'd like to send me a little something, like a five-pound bag.

    Sincerely yours,
    Ariel Frances Flack
    Not the mermaid

I...II...II..I.III...II...II..I.I.I.II.I.I..I....I.II

Chapter Sixteen

"The bus has spoken, and the bus is dead," Andre announces as he steps off the bus and joins me and the crowd standing around the side of the road, looking less than pleased.

There's a gray-brown burro about ten yards off giving me the evil eye. I'm thinking it's time to move on. "I don't have any carrots or whatever," I tell it. "I really don't."

"I'll push that bus if I have to," someone behind me mutters.

"You might have to," says my grandfather. "We *all* might have to."

Several backseat drivers are telling Lenny that it's his fault the bus overheated. Now a tow truck's going to have to come out from the nearest garage and move the bus, and then it'll need to be repaired.

"You should have gone around that line of cars," Grandpa tells Lenny with some authority, as if he's done it before.

"We could have killed a burro if I went around. No. Absolutely not. God's creatures," says Lenny.

We were on our way through Custer State Park after seeing Crazy

Horse, which is an amazing mountain carving like Mount Rushmore, only it was started later, didn't get government funding, and is still in progress. The nose, the profile, is gigantic, and the people walking all over look like little gnats from afar.

We only saw it from afar, because Lenny said that our entrance fee wasn't covered by our Leisure-Lee fee, so we had a bus vote to decide if we'd see it, and it was narrowly defeated, 23–21. I'm still mad about that, because it looked very cool.

So we were driving along the Wildlife Loop Road, where there are burros along the way that stop cars to beg for food, and people feed them, so we ended up sitting and waiting behind a line of cars. Then the bus overheated, blew a gasket or something, and we coasted, again, into the nearest business parking lot, which in this case was Happyland RV Park.

"Well, folks, this wasn't exactly what we were planning, now, was it?" asks Lenny, rubbing his hands together and looking slightly on edge. "Time to break out that emergency gear. Time for a taste of the outback!"

"There's an Outback around here? Really?" Andre's mom asks, her voice thick with hope. "I'd kill for some mashed potatoes."

"Oh, I just love their Blooming Onion. It's amazing," adds another passenger.

"It's just a blooming onion," Andre jokes.

"That's not Outback. That's Texas Roadhouse," someone else says.

"Folks! Folks. Pardon the interruption, but I'm sorry. I wasn't referring to the Outback steakhouse. I was talking about the out-back, camping out–wise," Lenny explains. "We'll be staying the night here."

Mrs. O'Neill's eyes widen. "Camping out? Oh no," she says. "I'll sleep on the bus before I lie on the ground."

"You can't sleep on the bus." Lenny shakes his head. "Against safety regulations."

"Well, so are rattlesnakes. I've never slept on the ground and I don't intend to start now. This was most definitely *not* in the brochure," she says, and everyone laughs.

"That disclaimer part about being able to roll with the punches. Didn't you read that, mate?" Lenny asks her, a twinkle in his eye, as if he's hilarious.

Mrs. O'Neill doesn't look amused in the slightest. "I'll roll and punch *you*," she tells him.

"Ma, lighten up. It's only camping," Andre says. "You've camped before."

"No, I haven't, and you haven't either," she says, "so quit pretending. We're not Boy Scouts." She raises one very nicely plucked eyebrow. "I'm not camping out here. You're breaking our agreement," she says to Lenny.

"Not really, because we did tell you to be ready for anything," Lenny replies. "And you can consider it an even exchange. You broke *our* agreement when you brought your pooch along."

She takes a step back. "Cuddles? He's not a pooch."

"Thoroughbred. Purebred. Whatever," Lenny says. "He's not on the passenger list. Cuddles O'Neill." Lenny runs his finger down an imaginary clipboard. "Nope. Not on here."

With that, he begins to pull out equipment, tents, and sleeping bags that we were all instructed to bring, but we didn't know why— I just remember Mom telling me to bring mine "in case of emergency." Uncle Jeff goes over to help, and loses his stamp hat on a tree branch that nearly takes out his eye.

"Look at all this," Lenny says. "You think any other bus tour gives you this?" He sweeps his arm around, indicating the outdoors, the view, the Happyland RV Park sign. "Not on your life."

I desperately look for a place where I can email Dylan. I see the campground office and decide to head over there, cash in hand, like only an addict would.

That night Andre and I grab a couple of s'mores and escape the campfire ghost stories that Lenny is telling. It's not even dark yet, so the campfire and the ghosts don't really have the same effect they would in an hour. We find a kind of quiet place and sit on a rock.

I can hear the faint, tinny sound of Andre's iPod through his headphones amid the crickets and other night sounds. He reaches over and hands me one of the earbuds. We just sit there without talking, which is weird because we always talk. I don't know what's different, but something is.

When the iPod dies, I hand him the earbud and he puts it in his pocket and we just sit there. Now I can hear the wind in the trees, and it's a really hot night. Just sitting there next to him, not even touching him, for some reason it's way more melty a situation than anything I've ever felt for Dylan.

It's not because it's a hundred degrees, although that kind of contributes.

It might be because he's putting his hand over mine and we are about to hold hands.

And then as my wrist turns to either hold his hand or push it away, I see on my Nike watch that it's nine o'clock, which is the time Dylan and I planned to IM.

I jump up, and then am really embarrassed that I did. "Sorry. Sorry. It's just that I told Dylan I'd write him at nine, so—"

"No, it's okay, go ahead," he says.

"I wasn't, um . . . you know." I don't even know what I'm trying to say.

"Yeah, I know."

So I sprint to the Happyland office, where the manager told me earlier that I could get online on her computer with my Hotmail account if I paid her five dollars. So I do, even though that seems kind of like highway robbery. I'm getting used to that, buying stuff at souvenir shops.

Dylan? You there? We're in Happyland.

Ariel? Where r u?

My heart starts pounding, and I don't know whether it's from the excitement of Dylan or the fact I ran so fast to get here. *He's there he's there he's there!*

It's an RV park. We're camping.

Oh yeah?

So I might not have much time. But can you come meet us?

What? R u crazy? I don't think so.

Y not?

2 far

Oh. R u sure?

Yeah

Come on, D, it wouldn't be that hard. We could take off and

Come on airel, be realistic

You misspelled my name

Oh

Again

Sorry

I don't want to be realistic, I'm sick of being realistic

u could come here and visit, maybe

how

I don't know. Anyway I wouldn't have time to hang out with you.

It just seems stupid to be this close and not see u

Yeah

But that's life I guess

Yeah

Did he always just say things like "yeah"? This is the most boring IM ever.

So see u in august

Or not. Right

Ok gtg

Bye

CU

But think about it okay?

If there's any chance at all

Do it

Escape

right

but you're not going to, are you?

probably not

ok

great

fantasterrific

what?

I walk out of the office and the screen door slams shut behind me, bouncing against its frame. I feel vaguely crushed. I'd been putting so much into this idea.

Andre is standing there, leaning against a tree. I can't believe he's waiting for me. "So was he there?"

It takes me a second, but I finally nod. "Yeah. He actually was."

"What did he say?"

"Um . . . not much."

"You guys going to meet up? Reconnoiter? Rendezvous?" Andre asks.

I shake my head. "I don't think so." I feel like really crying, only that's silly because nothing bad happened. But nothing good happened, either, and right now that's reason enough.

"No? No. So . . . California, then?" he asks.

There's a rumble of thunder above us, and dogs in the campsites begin to howl, or maybe they're wolves. "I'm not going to take that as a sign," says Andre, with a dejected look at the sky, which has finally darkened, and I see lightning flashing across it.

"I should probably go to my tent. Who are you sleeping with?" I ask.

"Excuse me, that's personal," he says.

I punch him lightly on the arm. "I meant, sharing a tent with. Or whatever."

"Dieter and Wolfgang. But I'm not sure if I know the password because it's German, so they might not let me in."

"You're kidding, right?"

There's another, louder rumble of thunder, and I wave good-bye and take off for our tent. I'm bunking with Mom, Zena, and Grandma in a four-person tent, which barely gives us enough room. It starts to rain, and within seconds it's raining harder, then harder still, drops attacking the tent from all sides, pinging and rolling onto the nylon fabric.

Andre's mom calls through our tent door, and before we can answer she unzips the door and starts to climb in. "Room for one more?" she asks. "I don't feel safe over there by myself. I thought I wanted privacy, but this camping is for the birds. Can you believe they bring us out here without decent shelter?"

She comes in and settles herself in the middle of us like we've known one another for years. She's wearing silk PJs, and Cuddles is in her arms, as usual. He looks terrified.

"So," Mrs. O'Neill says as she scoots down in her sleeping bag and covers Cuddles to calm him. "Here we are. It's not exactly what I planned."

"Me neither," I say, and so do Zena and Grandma. The only person not surprised seems to be Mom.

We listen to the pouring rain and talk about our favorite and not-so-favorite things on the trip so far. While everyone talks, I lie there and think about my disappointing IM with Dylan. I have to wonder: Do I really like him, or do I just like the idea of him? Did he just save me from yet another horrible school party where I was feeling left out? Maybe I only like him so much because I had a crush on him for so long that it became part of my genetic sequence.

Andre is more my type. But what's the point of getting involved with him? We don't even live close by *now*, never mind in the future.

After a while, as I'm mulling all this over, Grandma asks softly, but loudly enough to be heard over the downpour, "Can anyone else sleep in this racket? Because I can't."

"I'm awake," I whisper, waving to her in case she can't hear me, but then I realize she can't see me, either.

"Do you want to play backgammon?" she asks.

"Sure." I scoot over to sit on her sleeping bag and hang a flashlight from the roof while she gets out the game. She looks good even at midnight in a tent, with a stylish scarf over her short hair, and pink-and-red polka-dot flannel pajamas.

Everyone else is fast asleep. Mom is snoring, Zena is laughing in her sleep, and Andre's mom looks peaceful and serene, even though she's never camped or slept on hard ground before.

"Double or nothing?" Grandma asks after I lose the first game.

"Why not?" I say. I'm up for taking chances these days.

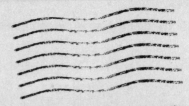

Sleep happy, stay happy, be happy. Our hookup, your trailer.

Happyland RV Park: "One Hookup for Life."

Gloves,

Tried sleeping with that infernal dog last night. Nowhere near as good as a cat. Didn't keep me as warm, plus slept on my head, plus does this annoying twitching thing in his sleep, like he's dreaming of chasing rabbits, which is silly because this dog is about ten times smaller than a rabbit.

How is your summer going? Have you caught many flies yet?

Wish you were here to share my pillow instead.

Your BFF,

Ariel

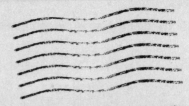

Chapter Seventeen

The next morning everything is wet, and we eat a breakfast of burned toast and leftover marshmallows and damp graham crackers. Or at least some people do. I opt for bottled water and an energy bar. Tents are hanging from trees to dry in the morning breeze. Sleeping bags are draped over bushes.

While we eat, we watch a tow truck hitching up the bus, which makes an awful groaning sound that must wake up every living thing in or near Happyland. Our luggage and all the stuff we had on the bus is sitting on the ground at our camp area.

Lenny comes by to pour "cowboy coffee," which tastes like burned cough syrup, and informs us that we'll all be going on a burro ride after breakfast. "We're going to be here a day or two, people. The bus can't be fixed, so we'll be getting a new one."

"And where's Jenny?" someone asks.

"Ah, yes, Jenny. She decided to take some R and R in Deadwood. Not to worry, we'll meet up with her later." Lenny tells us he's convinced a fellow Happyland camper to take him to town in his van so he can stock up on food and drink supplies. "It's all about going with the flow, people. Learning to adapt." He sounds extremely calm about our predicament.

Is it sick that I'm glad there's no bus, because then Mom can't tell me who to sit with?

"Lenny? I'll go to town with you," says Andre's mom. "I'll help buy the groceries."

"Lorraine, how sweet of you to help. Thank you, I'll take you up on that." Lenny bows to her.

"Help nothing, I need a day in civilization," she says as she goes to get her things ready.

"We could come help too," Andre offers. "Right, Ariel?" He nudges me, his elbow crashing against my ribs.

My mother chokes on her cowboy coffee. "I don't think that's a very good idea."

"Why not?"

"Well, uh—"

"We'll need the space for groceries. Sorry, kids, but thanks." Lenny surveys the crowd. "Now, who's going to volunteer for cleanup crew?"

My mother looks over at me and smiles, like she's achieved something.

"What did you think—we were going to run away?" Andre smiles and pinches my leg under the table.

"How fast do these things go, anyway?" my grandmother asks as she climbs onto her burro. He keeps sucking his teeth, like he just ate peanut butter, which makes him look a bit surly. He spits at the ground, then sucks his teeth again.

"Ma'am, have you ever been on a burro?" Mandy, one of the guides, asks her.

"I think I rode one about ten years ago in the Grand Canyon. At least my butt remembers," she says, and Zena, Mom, and I all laugh.

"Don't you have any jeans, or some thicker pants?" Mandy asks, surveying Grandma's pink *velour du jour* tracksuit.

"Sorry. This is how she rides," jokes Zena.

Grandma goes sort of cantering off, her surly burro slightly out of control. "What do I do?" she turns around to ask. "What do I do?"

"Hold on, woman; I'll be right there!" Grandpa calls, urging his burro to catch up to her.

"I usually travel by bike," Uncle Jeff tells Mandy as she helps him get onto one of the horses on the lot.

"Really?" Mandy asks politely.

"Harley," he says, puffing out his chest a little. He's trying to impress her, so he doesn't tell her that this was at least ten years ago. "Now, what's the difference between a burro and a burr-ee-toe?" he asks as he sets off, following Grandma and Grandpa across the field toward a trail.

"Should a person drink cowboy coffee and then go on a long ride?" an older woman riding behind me asks.

"How do you drive this thing?" her husband jokes.

"Where are my spurs?" Ethel adds. "Are spurs extra?"

After about twenty minutes, everyone who hadn't already left before me and Andre starts to pass us. We have the slow burros, the ones who've been ground down by the boredom, like us.

"Hey, guys!" Wolfgang says as he ambles by on the right.

"*Wiedersehen!*" Dieter calls over his shoulder as his horse goes galloping past on the left.

"How did he rate a horse?" I ask.

"He's tall? Or maybe he threatened to sing 'SexyBack' again," Andre says. *"Fee I pee . . ."*

"Don't," I say, laughing.

We let everyone pass us, because this isn't a race. We have all day to kill, even if the burros are only a three-hour rental. Andre suggests we take a detour. I point out that we'll lose the group if we do that.

"No, we won't," he says. "These animals are slow."

"Right. Especially *ours*. So how will we catch up?"

"We'll leave a trail of Skittles to find our way back."

"That's dumb," I say.

"But it'll work. Come on, try it."

I reach into my little backpack. But my burro leans to the opposite side and I wobble, and the Skittles bag slips from my hand. "Oh, shoot. I dropped the bag." I tell my burro to stop, which is easy for him because he didn't like moving much anyway. I get off carefully, holding the reins.

Andre stops beside me, but just sits up on his burro, watching me.

"Aren't you going to come down?" I ask.

"Sure. Of course. Definitely," he says. But he eyes the ground and then eyes the burro's neck, and looks around at its legs, its hooves. "How do you, uh, get off these things?"

"Just swing your leg over," I say.

"But what if he panics and throws me to the ground?"

"He's not Seabiscuit. He's a burro. Or she. Whatever," I say. "They're tame." I go and stand by his burro, and sort of put my hand on its flank to keep it from moving.

Andre slides off, into my arms, and we totally crash to the ground. Me cushioning his fall. In other words me, on the ground underneath Andre. Burros above us. Not running away. Not even caring.

Here's their moment of freedom and they don't budge.

I look away from them and up at Andre. He's not budging, either. *He's lying on top of me.*

"Here. I think you dropped this," he says, and he picks up a grape Skittle from the assortment on the ground and tries to put it into my mouth.

"That was on the ground. Ew." I look at him. This camping thing is making me desperate in more ways than one. That was my last bag of candy. My pulse is pounding in my ears, because Andre is *lying on top of me.* I can't breathe so well. It seems like everything that's happened between us so far is nothing compared to this.

"Are you going to eat it or not?" He pushes it against my lips.

"Quit it," I say, but it comes out sounding like "Mm-mm." I shake my head, and he pops the candy into his mouth, then kisses me, so I can taste the grape, too.

We start to make out right there, which is totally stupid and crazy and at the same time fun and exciting, and I'm melting as fast as that grape Skittle that is no more.

We stop for a second, and I look him in the eye. "This isn't cool. You don't want a girlfriend."

"No?"

"No, you don't. You said that. Really rudely, actually."

"Right." He kisses me again. "And then there's the matter of Dylan, who you're dying to see—"

I kiss him. "Right. I was. Which makes this—"

"Wrong." He kisses me. "Taboo." Kiss. "Not on the list of scheduled stops." Kiss.

"Actually they're . . ." Kiss. "Unscheduled . . ." I say. Kiss. "Stops."

Somewhere above me I hear a throat being cleared. Again. Louder. Still louder.

Then it's a cough and a hack, like someone choked on a piece of hard candy.

We unlock lips and I look up, and the sun nearly blinds me because of course my sunglasses fell off when I crashed to the ground.

"I think you two may have lost the trail," says Uncle Jeff, towering over us, looking sort of like a large knight on his steed.

He's holding a walking stick that could be taken as a sword, if you were far away and had poor eyesight. His floppy hat with a hundred laminated stamp buttons and pins on it is glinting in the bright sun and could be seen as a helmet.

It could also be seen as clashing with his three gold necklaces.

"Uh, oops!" I say, kind of too loudly.

We both stand up, brushing needles and dirt and bark from our clothes.

"You should have seen these crazy burros," Andre says.

"Oh yeah. They went totally wild," I add. "Threw us off."

Uncle Jeff looks at the burros, who are eating the dropped Skittles off the ground. More than tame, they're resigned.

"Why don't you try to handle them, and get back on?" Uncle Jeff suggests. He's not smiling.

Andre steps on a large rock to get onto his burro, while I climb up, dragging myself onto the poor animal. Once I'm back on I adjust my watch, which has gotten all twisted around.

"Let's go. I'll bring up the rear," Uncle Jeff says, and I try not to laugh, but then Andre snickers and I lose it.

We ride along the trail, Andre first, then me, then Uncle Jeff. When we catch up to the group on a scenic overlook, Zena ambles over to me. "Forget what I said, A."

"Which time?" I ask.

"About him being weird. He's not," Zena says, admiring Andre from behind. "He's totally cute."

I know, I think. "Great. Glad you think so. But we're just friends."

"Really? So I could ask him out?"

"No, Z, because you're twelve."

"Shut up," she says.

"You're twelve, as in twelvery young."

"And you're sixteen, as in sixtremelyannoyingteen."

"Well, so is he," I tell her. "He's going to be a senior, and no way are you asking out a high school senior."

"I've done it before," she says with a shrug. "It's no big deal."

"Where was this?" I ask.

"Wall Drug. Didn't you *see* us with those guys?"

"No." I lower my sunglasses and stare at her. "You almost picked up a guy at Wall Drug?"

She shrugs.

"That's dangerous, okay? Don't do that," I say. "Really, Z. Don't."

"But it's okay for you to make out with Andre," she says.

"Make out? I've . . . I've never—"

"No, but you thought about it," she says.

Of course, I *have* done it, and I've thought about it ever since. "You're twelvexing. You know that?"

"Oh yeah? Well, you're sixteeny-tiny."

I laugh. "I'm what?"

"I'll keep it realsimple from now on, so you won't get confused. But if you guys do make out, *tell* me." She nudges her burro with her heels and takes off to catch up with Bethany.

"Right. Like I would!" I call after her.

Actually, I wish I could tell somebody. But that's not exactly the kind of thing you put on a postcard—and definitely not to your cat back home.

When Lenny and Mrs. O'Neill get back with the groceries, there's a minor emergency—or actually, a big emergency about a small thing. Mrs. O'Neill thought Andre had Cuddles, while Andre thought *she* had Cuddles.

So nobody actually had Cuddles. And Cuddles probably thought . . . everyone had deserted him in the wilderness.

Everyone in the group splits up to look for him, even the ones who never wanted him along on the trip. We spend all afternoon calling his name, hunting for him.

When he hasn't been found by nightfall, Andre is pacing by the campfire. I'm trying to keep him company, but Andre is so stressed that he can't quite listen to me without getting upset.

Mrs. O'Neill is inside our tent, praying, with Mom and Grandma sitting by her side, consoling her in between random calls of "Cuddles! Come back, sweetheart!"

I tell Andre that his jeans are slipping down—he wears them low but these are too low, and his underwear is showing more than usual. I go over and try to playfully adjust them, and he bats my hand away.

"I'm dealing with a lot of stuff right now. My butt is the least of my problems."

"Okay, but I just thought—"

"What? In the missing-dog posters, my underwear might be showing?" he asks. "This is another thing my mom's going to hold against me. Just watch. I mean, someone stole him, obviously. And it's my fault because I was thinking about you, or maybe that makes this your fault. Instead of listening to her tell me to watch him, and— you know what?" Andre turns to me and takes a swig from a bottle of water. "The fact that he's missing. It's a sign."

"It is?" I ask.

"Yes. It's a sign that we're supposed to run off tonight too. We're supposed to follow his lead."

"Right," I say.

"What?"

I don't know what makes me say the next thing, probably stress, but it comes out meaner than I intend. "Andre, did you notice that you constantly talk about running away, but only Cuddles has the guts to do it?" It's supposed to be a joke, but it's one of those jokes that has too much truth in it.

Andre looks at me like he wishes there were two buses, one to put me on and one to put him on. Like he'd rather be anywhere else in the world.

"You know what? You were right," he says. "What you said earlier today. I don't want a girlfriend, and I don't want to like you."

"I don't want to like you either," I say. "You just happen to be here."

"Oh, really? I just 'happen' to be here. Well, no kidding. This wasn't my plan. And what, you'd rather be spending time with the infamous Dylan, who by the way left you for the entire summer, or haven't you noticed?"

Tears sting my eyes just as Uncle Jeff's voice pierces the darkness. "Found him!"

Everyone runs toward Uncle Jeff as he emerges from the woods, saying, "Got him! Call off the dogs! Sorry, didn't mean that." He nuzzles Cuddles's chin with his finger. "You're so little I could carry you in my postal satchel and nobody would be the wiser. Together we'd show those flying rodents a thing or two."

He hands Cuddles to Mrs. O'Neill, who starts weeping with happiness. It's embarrassing.

"I told you, Ma. I told you we'd find him," says Andre.

"Wh-where was he?" she asks.

"Found him over at that campsite, dragging a Pop-Tarts wrapper around, trying to dig a hole," Uncle Jeff says. "I thought it was a squirrel at first. So naturally I kept my distance." His face turns sort of red. "Anyway. Just glad I could help."

Mrs. O'Neill hugs Cuddles and offers him liver treats. "Who's my favorite boy?" she keeps saying. Then she looks up at Andre. "I can't believe you let this happen."

"Ma! It wasn't . . . he's not . . . You know what? Forget it," Andre says. "You should have bought Cuddles a seat on this trip—not me." He stalks off down the small road that winds through the campground. He's gone. I'm out of Skittles, and he's gone.

Why did I have to say that to him? Like he wasn't having a bad enough night already?

I feel horrible, so I decide to get ready for bed and try to forget this entire night. I grab my cosmetic bag from the tent and go over to the water pump to brush my teeth.

My mother comes over while I'm midrinse. I don't know where she comes from, but it's like an owl swooping out of a tree. "Ariel, we have to talk," she says. "And I'd prefer that we get it over with tonight."

I shake out my toothbrush and rinse my face with the cold water a few times, drying it on the bottom of my sweatshirt. "That sounds ominous." What else can go wrong tonight?

"It's not. But . . . look, Ariel. What I've been trying to say for the past few days . . . We are *going* to move," she says. "For sure. I'm sorry. I didn't know how to tell you. I've been trying and trying, but you don't want to listen to me."

"No," I say, twisting my bag in my hands, then shoving it underneath one arm and preparing to walk off. "We can't. I can't."

"We have to," she says.

"You want to leave Dad, fine. You did that already," I say.

"I want to leave that whole chapter of our lives behind," she says. "I don't want to see people pitying me, or us. I don't want to bump into them at the grocery store."

"So we'll leave our neighborhood a little," I suggest. "We'll move a few miles away, find a new store."

"I'm talking about leaving the state, Ariel. We need distance. My professional reputation is suffering. You can understand that."

"But, Mom, I'm not going to leave Sarah and all of my friends. And I've worked so hard to be part of the team. I've got people who totally believe in me," I say.

She shrugs. "You'll stay in touch with Sarah. And as far as running, if you're good there, you'll be even better somewhere else."

She doesn't understand. She's never understood. "What about Grandma and Grandpa Flack?"

"Yes, you'd miss them. So would I. But what about *my* parents? We've never lived close to them. We were going up there for two weeks, anyway, right? You'll help pick out the neighborhood, the house. We'll make sure it has everything you want. We'll get a location with a good school, great running team—there are coaches who would die to have you on their team."

"But I already have a coach," I say. "And where we're going . . . Dad won't be there. At all."

Mom shakes her head. "No. I can't see that he will be."

As uncomfortable as things are between us sometimes, do I really only want to see him on major holidays? "Are your parents behind all this?" I ask. I've loved spending this time with Grandma and Grandpa, but it's starting to feel like a conspiracy.

"Who do you think has been helping us out? Do you think I just walked out into the backyard and found money growing on the trees? It's my parents. I need them right now—you need them, too. I mean, sure, I have a career and we'll build on that, but I can't do it on my own," Mom says.

"Well, I'm not moving," I say.

"Yes. You are," she replies. "We are."

"Jujyfruit?" Uncle Jeff offers, shaking the box as he walks up to us at the pump, completely clueless to the fact that Mom and I have just had this major blowout.

"No!" I say. Then I change my mind and take the entire box out of his hand.

As I do, there's a *putt-putt* sound getting closer and closer to our group site. Giant headlights turn into our parking area, and gradually I can make out that it's the old red-and-white Leisure-Lee bus pulling up.

Everyone climbs out of their tents, in pajamas, wearing curlers, or missing dentures.

We all stand in suspense as the door opens with a long, slow hiss.

"Welcome aboard!" Lee says, tipping his cowboy hat to us.

Buffalo of South Dakota
The bison is the biggest land animal in the U.S. Buffalo roam free by the hundreds in Custer State Park. Warning: Do not approach. Appreciate from a distance.

Dylan,

We're staying at Custer State Park, or as my uncle calls it, Custard State Park. Like it's Culver's and he's going to order a turtle sundae.

There is lots of wildlife—no turtles though.

I stop writing. This is pathetic. I've sent him a dozen postcards and none of them has been any good or said anything important.

He doesn't care, and the last thing he wrote that was interesting was probably my email address. He doesn't spell my name right. Ever.

I could even forgive that, because it's not a common name.

Only now that I've met Andre, I realize Dylan and I don't really have much. He's never asked about my dad. He's mostly only talked about himself.

Still, I can't bring myself to tell him that we're moving. He'll forget about me even more, and we're not even gone yet, but by the time he gets home from camp we probably will be. That good-bye grope, on the green-and-yellow Packers beanbag chair, that was it for us.

Life never gives you enough advance warning. On anything.

Chapter Eighteen

The next morning, Lee insists on driving, and it's frightening.

Not because he's older and slower. It's the opposite. He's done the route so many times that he bombs down the road without using the brakes. He takes the curves too quickly. Lenny drops his microphone twice before he gets a chance to say anything. He's flopping around the bus aisle like a passenger on a turbulent flight.

"This is known as the Pins and Needles Highway," Lenny says.

"No, it isn't. This is Iron Mountain Road," Lee corrects him, glancing over his shoulder as he takes a tight turn.

"Yes. Ahem." Lenny coughs. "Right, you're right, Lee, of course. Well, maybe I misspoke because I'm on pins and needles here," he says, "waiting for the exciting views of Mount Rushmore."

"Lenny, be quiet and let them enjoy the scenery for a change," Lee says.

Lenny falls into a seat and isn't heard from again.

The views through little stone arches over the road are truly incredible. It actually is breathtaking, the way Lenny said it would be. It's Mount Rushmore the way I've always seen it in photos, but in miniature. But to be fair, we are rushing it, or Lee is, anyway. I think the speed limit may have changed since the last time he drove this route. I expect him to send cars hurtling off the road in our wake.

There are oohs and aahs.

"This is just fantasterrific." Uncle Jeff sighs beside me. I kind of want to agree, except I still hate that made-up word. I glance up ahead to see where Andre's sitting, to see how many words he has for this view. He's staring straight ahead and frowning, as if he has something else on his mind. There's so much tension on the bus right now—between him and me, between him and his mom, and between me and my mom—that it could probably power the other bus's busted engine all on its own.

We get closer and closer. Finally we drive up a long and winding hill, past lots of cars and traffic, which takes forever because we didn't get an early start. And then we're there. The parking lot at Mount Rushmore. The granite faces loom above us and can't quite be believed.

"You have to experience it before you hit the gift shop," Andre says as we walk up onto the memorial's avenue of flags and I start to automatically peel off to the left when I see the gift shop.

We never made up, officially, after last night, but we're talking again. I have no idea how things stand between us. I love the fact that my last bag of Skittles was sacrificed to the ground, because of what it made us do. But when I think about it and him, I don't know how I'm supposed to feel now. Guilty? Happy? Like that was then, and this is now?

"No, I have to hit the gift shop and get postcards," I tell him. "Then I can write them while I sit outside and look at the faces."

He shakes his head. "Obsessed."

"Yeah, well. It'll only take me a second. You can wait out here and think of two more ways to insult me," I say.

"Hurry. It won't take me long," he promises.

I walk into the giant shop, overwhelmed by the choices. There isn't just one postcard rack; there are several. I don't know where to begin, so I go clockwise. Except that it's sort of an angular place.

I'm looking at the big cards first, comparing buffalo and state shapes and Rushmore trivia, when I hear someone say, "Ariel?"

That voice.

I nearly fall over.

It's my dad.

"Ha! I knew I'd see you first. Got here early just in case." He steps around the postcard rack and gives me a big hug. He's wearing an old tee and his faded Levi's and he looks thin and really relaxed, the way he always did on our road trips when he didn't have to shave and wear a tie every day and all that work stuff.

But he doesn't look exactly the same as the last time I saw him. He looks scruffier.

"So," he says. "How's things?"

How's things? Is that all he's going to say? What is he doing here? I shrug. "Okay, if you like bus tours."

"And things of that nature?" he says, and I know I'm supposed to laugh like I usually do because he's making fun of Uncle Jeff, but I can't make myself.

I start to feel nervous. I want to know why he's here, but I'm afraid to ask. "You want to go outside? You want to, um, explain why you're here?"

"What's to explain? We always wanted to see Rushmore, didn't we?" Dad puts his arm around my shoulder as we leave the store. I feel myself pulling him to the edge, not of the cliff but of the avenue of flags, because I'm hoping to shield him from Mom, and vice versa.

"So here we are," he says. "Is it like you pictured?"

"Not exactly," I say. See, in my vision, we all came here together, in a car. And my parents weren't divorced and my dad wasn't a pseudo-criminal who got off for lack of state's evidence.

"No?"

"No. It's, um, bigger." I look over at him. "How did you know we'd be here today? This morning?"

"I've actually been here since yesterday, trying to meet up with you guys. Where's your sister?"

"Oh, she's around, definitely. I wonder where," I say, scanning the dozens of people milling around, admiring the sculpted presidents' faces.

Andre somehow manages to find us in the crowd, and I'm thrilled, overjoyed, grateful to see him. "Funny. I don't see anyone I can relate to up there," he says, pointing up at Mount Rushmore. "Where's Martin Luther King?"

"I think they carved this in the forties," I point out.

"Figures. So, there's not *more* mountain up there to carve? There's room," he says, looking back at the monument. "If they can make Crazy Horse, then they can make Dr. King."

I smile at him, so glad he's here to defuse this really weird situation, even if he does it by creating one of his own. "Dad, this is my friend Andre."

"Hey, how's it going? Andre, like Agassi?"

Andre looks at me and we both roll our eyes. "Yes, that's it exactly, Dad."

Andre walks closer to the monument itself, and we follow him.

"You've been hanging out with Ariel, then you must be cool."

"Pretty much," Andre says.

"So is there anyone up there you *can* relate to?" I ask. "And let me tell you. There aren't any women up there, either, okay?"

"Maybe I can relate to Lincoln. But he was weird, right? He had psychological problems," Andre comments.

"No wonder you relate to him," I say.

"Oh! Oh! Prepare to be rushed at Rushmore." He wraps his arms around my waist and lifts me up to carry me and toss me over the edge while my dad looks at us, seeming a little left out. It's only going to get worse, I realize as Andre sets me down, because I see my mom headed in our direction.

"Richard," she says to him. "What on earth are you doing here?" She doesn't yell or curse, and I kind of admire her for that. I glance at her hand to see if she's wearing her ring that was rescued from under the bus, and she isn't, even after all that rescue effort. Which says something. And also makes her hand look smaller and kind of strangely naked.

"Hey, there! Sorry I couldn't let you know; you guys don't have any way of being contacted, so . . . anyway. Family summer road trip." He shrugs and shoves his hands into his pockets, kind of like a little kid would do. "Seemed like a good tradition we should keep up."

Mom doesn't look like she agrees with any part of what he's just said.

"Um . . . this might seem like an obvious question, but how did you know we'd be here today? At right this second?" Mom asks.

He shrugs. "I took a chance."

Mom looks like there can't possibly be enough miles between them. "I bet you did," she says.

Dad laughs. "No, actually I called the bus company. You told me what it was called in your postcards," he says to me.

"P-p-postcards?" Mom sputters. "Really."

I imagine the look on my grandfather's face when he sees Dad, and how he'll probably chase him all the way out of the state, how he and Uncle Jeff will devise a plot to trip up Dad, how my grandmother might put down a slick layer of nail polish and hair spray for him to wipe out on. They'll team up against him.

Where *are* they, anyway? I need help here. I try to signal to Andre, to say something like, "Save me!" with one look.

He appears frightened by my expression, but he gets it. "Mrs., um, Timmons. My mom wants to treat you to lunch," Andre says, and he somehow manages to drag my mother away, her fists clenched under her Custer State Park sweatshirt sleeves.

"Timmons?" my dad mutters, and I decide not to get into that conversation, not yet.

Dad starts goofing around, posing in front of the presidents' faces, as if I'm supposed to take pictures of him and we can laugh about them later. I wish I could laugh now, because this is really bizarre, but I just spent miles and miles getting away from him and the problems he created for us back home. And getting away wasn't a bad thing. As much as I love him, it was not a bad thing.

"Am I more a Lincoln or a Roosevelt?" he asks.

Not that I'm a presidential expert, but he's so unlike any of them. His pose reminds me more of a mug shot than anything else. There are these giant majestic faces of these great men, and then my dad.

So then I do take his picture, to make sure I'll remember. He looks a little disheveled, like perhaps he used his last dollar to get here, and slept in the car, or something like that. He has little cuts on his face, as if he shaved with an old razor at a rest stop. I wouldn't recognize this kind of stuff except I've seen some things in the past week, camping and roughing it and stopping at questionable rest areas, that I wouldn't have known about before.

"Well?" he prompts as all these things go through my head, and the wind won't stop blowing super hard, whipping my hair into my face, blowing the flags around us so it's almost hard to hear each other.

"You're more a Nixon," I say, and I only know this from one of Lenny's dumb games to pass the time while the bus was broken down, called Name the President.

"Ha-ha," Dad says.

"So, Dad. How did you get here, really, and why are you here?"

He looks taken aback, as if this is an absurd question, as if his being at Mount Rushmore isn't the thing that's absurd.

"Well, you have to admit it's a little strange. I mean, we'll be home in a few weeks," I tell him. "You could have talked to us then."

He shakes his head. "Not back there. Everything's . . . cloudy back there. I need to be on the road to sort things out. On the toad, rather."

He waits for me to laugh, but I don't. "And . . ." I prompt.

"You know how it is; you know how I'm always happier when I'm on an adventure."

I don't comment, because what I used to think of as his "adventures" maybe aren't so fun anymore.

"But, Dad," I say, thinking how strange it is that both he and Mom want to get away in order to make things work, but work in different ways. "What did you want to sort out?"

"Isn't it obvious?" He gazes up at the sun above, takes a deep breath. "I'm here to talk with your mother and see if I can work things out with her."

"Dad, you can't."

"What?"

"Talk with her," I tell him. "Or work things out."

"Why not?"

"It's too late."

"How can it be too late? We were together seventeen years, Ariel. That's not something you just toss away."

"Isn't it?" I say back. "I mean, isn't that what you did?"

Zena suddenly runs up and throws her arms around him, and I wish I could still do that, but I can't. Because I'm not twelve anymore. And not being twelve means knowing things that aren't necessarily things you want to know, that your dad's losing it a little bit, maybe more so now than he was before. That instead of pulling it together like you wish, he's headed in the other direction.

"But you don't have a car. So how did you get here?" asks Zena, curious in the same kind of way that I am.

"They have bus tours for everything, from everywhere. I got a cheap one to Deadwood, and then—"

"Of course you did," I say. "The gambling express, right?"

Dad looks shocked.

"We were there, Dad. Didn't see you at the casino, but then, there are lots to choose from."

"Ariel, I didn't go there to gamble," he says. "I couldn't get a decent flight to Rapid City, so Lee told me to fly to Scottsbluff and get a shuttle."

"Lee?" I ask.

"I called him. He also thought there could be an empty seat on the bus; maybe I could take it."

"No. There aren't any extra seats," I say quickly, because isn't this trip hard enough without adding Dad to the mix?

"Isn't there one?" says Zena. "The new bus has a few more rows of seats. We could bring it to a bus vote or something."

"That's what we do," I explain. "We have these bus votes. Really dumb, but, you know. Fair. Democratic. Majority rule and all."

"But hey, if there's no room on the bus, I want you all to come with me," says Dad earnestly. He puts his arm around me and squeezes.

That's when I smell it. That lemon-lime casino scent. The towelette. I smell it, and I want to punch him in the stomach.

I could ask, and he could tell me that it's restroom soap, but I know it isn't.

I could ask, and he could tell me it was something he got from a restaurant, the kind they give you after you eat a rack of ribs.

But that's not it.

I know where it's from.

And if I asked if it was from a casino, he'd have some story at the ready, about how he ran in just to use the phone.

The fact that he's still gambling doesn't make him an awful person. It just makes him . . . not reliable.

I need reliable.

"We'll rent a car, we'll get off the beaten path, we'll just see what happens, where we want to go," he's saying.

But we can't do that anymore—or maybe he still can, but I can't. If he's going to come all this way to find us, but still be hitting casinos, then I don't know what to say to him—at all.

No comment?

Sarah,

Everything is so screwed up right now. Dad's here, at Mount Rushmore. And we're moving.

Not on the bus, mind you.

We're moving moving.

This sucks.

This postcard sucks.

Miss you.

Love,

AF

Before I mail it, I look at it again, and then I rip the postcard up and throw it out. One of the pieces misses the national monument trash can. I don't care. I watch it get blown away by the blustery wind, bouncing down the avenue of flags. The next thing you know it'll be sucked into the air and wind, and bounce off Roosevelt's glasses or Lincoln's nose.

Let someone else find it for once. Found objects are overrated, but let them discover that.

You know that expression, being at your wit's end?

I'm apparently there.

Chapter Nineteen

There's no bus vote to decide whether Dad can join us, but Mom brings it to a family vote. We've gotten a hall pass for the night, and we're at a "family restaurant." As a family. One big, weird, dysfunctional family. They should clear the restaurant when they see us coming.

Except Dad isn't with us. Mom asked him to "respect our space" and give us time to talk this over. I don't want to talk it over. I don't know what we should do.

"You should carb up for the race tomorrow," my grandmother says when she sees me picking at my side salad. "Have some of these rolls." She passes a basket to me and won't set it down until I take one and butter it.

My grandfather is having spaghetti with extra bread sticks, and my uncle, king of the strip steak, is eating a salad. "A salad?" I ask, pointing to it.

"Don't want to be bogged down." He pats his belly.

"Right," I say. "Good plan."

"So, Zena, Ariel. What do you think?" Mom asks after we've all had a few bites of dinner. Like she *wants* us to get indigestion.

"That my cheeseburger needs more ketchup," says Zena.

"That I don't actually like honey-mustard dressing after all," I say.

"Try ketchup," Zena offers.

"On a salad?"

Mom clears her throat after polishing off a hot fudge sundae and before digging into her main meal, fettuccine Alfredo. The blood in her arteries must be slower moving than the traffic on the road up to Mount Rushmore. "I meant, about your father."

"Oh," I say.

"Sure," says Zena.

"I will listen to you guys," Mom says. "If you tell me you want to go with him, then we will, or you will, and I'll stay here. Which will be really hard for me to do. But okay."

"I don't want to leave Bethany," Zena says.

And I *do* want to leave, I think, but not with Dad. "I, um, don't think it would be a great idea. You know how it is when you come into a theater or the living room and everyone else is in the middle of watching a movie? It'd be like that for him."

"So, is that a 'no' on inviting Dad onto the bus?" asks Mom, ready to wrap this up before we've even really discussed it.

"Yes. It's a no," I say.

"Right," Zena agrees, and I'm very relieved she agrees, but I can't help wondering why she does so quickly, when she seemed so thrilled to see him earlier.

"Well, then. How about going with him? On another trip?" Mom can barely choke the words out, I can tell. She's been twisting the same piece of fettuccine around her fork for the last three minutes.

"Does he even have a car?" Grandpa wants to know.

"Sure," says Zena.

"A *decent* car?" asks Uncle Jeff. "One that can get you from here to there?"

"He didn't drive here. That's all I know," I say. "So we'd have to rent a car."

"Rent a car." My mother coughs, that piece of fettuccine finally having gone down—the wrong way. "With his credit record, good luck."

"Mom? Not seeing any personal growth here," I comment. "You talked badly about him when we left home and you're still doing it."

She looks a bit taken aback by my comment, but she nods. "The purpose of this dinner is to give you guys a voice."

"So you're including us in *this* decision. But not in the moving one," I point out. "Zena? Listen. We're actually moving. I mean, aren't you furious? How can you just sit there?" I look over at my grandparents and uncle. "No offense, you guys. This is just . . . it's *news* to me. Brand-new news."

Zena turns to me, and her face for once looks older to me and slightly harsh, except she has a tiny drop of ketchup in the corner of her mouth that reminds me she's still Zena. "Ariel, I *can't* be furious. About anything. If I start being mad? It wouldn't stop. And it wouldn't help."

"But you're with me, right?" I ask. "You don't want to move. You'd have to leave your friends—"

"Half my friends ended up being jerks to me anyway," she says. "Do you know how many things I was suddenly not invited to this past spring?"

I think about it. "Yeah. I kind of know what you mean. But I just feel like we're running from our problems."

"Oh, really, and you don't do that? Anyway, making new friends isn't that hard. What about you and Andre?"

Uncle Jeff starts to cough. "A good guy. Andre. Good guy."

I hope they don't notice that my face is turning red, that I'm remembering him, and me, and him *on* me. I change the subject as quickly as I can. "Gloves. What about Gloves?" I ask. "She won't know where to come home to. She'll get lost, Z."

"She has that cat sense of smell. She'll figure it out," says Zena.

"She won't have her favorite window ledge anymore to lie on in the sun. That cat across the street. Oliver. They'll miss hissing at each other."

Zena just stares at me and raises her eyebrows. "I think she'll adjust, A."

Maybe she will, I think. *But what about me?* I could say that I wouldn't leave town, that I'd stay and live with Dad, only I can't. I know that. I guess I knew it before, but for some reason, now that I've seen him here, seen his road persona again, seen how he's a little nervous and unhinged, I know it even more than before.

"So. Have we voted?" Mom asks.

Grandma suddenly drops her spoon into her empty soup bowl with a clatter. Her face is bright red, like she's going to burst. I'm about to ask if she's okay when she says, "*We?* It's not up to us, Tamara. It's up to *them.*" She points at me and Zena.

"Well, I'm sorry!" says Mom, tossing down her napkin.

"Here's what's going to happen, girls," Grandma goes on. "You'll come to visit us; you'll see what you think. Not everything has to be decided tonight, or on this trip. Give them a break! They've had enough to deal with. This is supposed to be their vacation, for goodness' sake!" She stands up, pushing her chair back, grabs her purse, and bolts for the ladies' room. Zena is right behind her.

Mom leaves, but doesn't head for the restroom—she goes straight outside. Uncle Jeff follows her.

That leaves me and Grandpa. I look awkwardly at him, but his face is stoic, even in the midst of this. Looking at him makes me think about my track coach, whether she really believes in me much or not, whether the team would care if I moved away. I think about all the offhand, rude comments from people, about how I feel like I have to prove myself over and over again. The newspaper article taped to my locker. *No comment.*

It doesn't take anything to become disliked. I mean, you can wear the wrong shirt one day and you're suddenly on the outs.

And this is so much more than that.

Whenever I see Dad now I just can't like being there, because I can't stop thinking about this stuff and how it's affecting me every day of my life. I make nice and talk to him, but the whole time I'm burning up inside.

I can't spend much time with him until he works on things long enough to get them right. I hate that I think this, because it sounds like something my mother would say, in fact, *has* said. I don't want to agree with her, on principle, because she can be awfully preachy and condescending about this stuff, but she's right.

It's not like the problem just started at Christmas. It started a long time before that, and just built until it reached a crisis point.

My grandfather looks like he wants to say something, but he can't. Maybe it's because Grandma told him to be quiet. Finally he says, "Would you mind going to check on them?"

"Sounds like a good idea." I stand up and walk to the back of the restaurant and into the restroom. Zena's blowing her nose, and Grandma is standing in front of the mirror, reapplying her eye makeup, because clearly they've both been crying.

"Maybe he is too old for you," Grandma is saying, "but are you at least learning any German?"

"My favorite word is *schlecht*," Zena replies.

"What's that?"

"Not good," Zena says as she opens the restroom door, striding out without even acknowledging me. "Crappy. Crummy."

We get back to the motel, where Dad was supposed to meet us at eight. He isn't there. We wait and wait. Finally our room phone rings.

"Dad?" I say as I answer it.

"No, Andre," he says. "You're out of Skittles, right?"

"Yes, actually," I tell him. "It's Andre," I whisper to Mom and Zena, though I wonder why I just admitted that to Mom.

"Can you meet me in the lobby?" he asks.

I look at Mom. "I don't know," I say.

"Come on, please. You've got to save me. My mom's talking about signing us up for the next Leisure-Lee trip—like, the one that starts the day after this one ends. I think it goes to Arizona. She and Lee spent a little too much time together at the cocktail lounge tonight. She just went down to the lobby to meet him and a bunch of other people for a nightcap."

"You're kidding," I say, sitting on the edge of the bed.

"No. I wish," he says. "Come on, Ariel. I know I was a jerk the other night, but you've got to come with me. It's the plan, you know? I won't make it to L.A. without you."

"You have a point," I say.

"So are you in?" he asks.

I look over at my mom, because she's making frantic signals at me and I don't understand them. "Ariel. Get off the phone! You've talked long enough. We need to keep the line clear."

"Why?" I ask her.

"Your father's probably trying to call, to explain why he's late," she says.

"Sure, Mom," I say. "I'm sure he is."

I sigh and flop back on the bed, looking up at the ceiling. Being on a real bed after camping for two nights feels so nice. Do I really want to trade it for a few questionable nights on the road?

Mom stands over me, holding out her hand for the phone. "Andre, I have to get going," I say. "But I'll see you for that early run we talked about."

"Early run?" he asks.

"Before the marathon—you know, the warm-up jog you're going on with me and the rest of the group. Meet me outside at six."

"Six?" He sounds as if he is nearly choking.

"Good night!" I say cheerfully.

"I didn't know Andre was a runner," my mom comments as I hand her the phone.

"Oh. Well, he is." I nod.

Black Hills Buffalo Barbecue & Co.
We kill it, you grill it.
Buses welcome.

Mom,

Don't worry about me. Andre and I will be together and I've got some money and we can take care of ourselves. I'll be safe. I'll be real safe.

But I'm leaving because I just can't stand everything.

I don't want to stay where we are, and I don't want to move.

When I figure it out, I'll be back.

Love,

Ariel

Chapter Twenty

In the morning I get dressed to go running. I'll play it cool to my mom if she rolls over and wakes up, tell her I'm going out for a jog like every other morning. But of course she doesn't wake up, because she's not that kind of sleeper. She's the kind who needs three alarms just to get her attention.

I went down earlier this morning to stash my backpack in a bush on the edge of the parking lot, across from the lobby. I'm like that soccer-playing girl in *Bend It Like Beckham*. I've also left a note for Andre under his room door about where to meet me, for real.

I leave the postcard on the motel bathroom sink, but then I read it again and decide, no, I'm not leaving it. I'll figure out another way to get in touch. I throw it out, but then picture Mom searching the room and finding that, and it's not very good and doesn't really tell her anything. So I stuff the postcard under the waistband of my running shorts. As I do, the hundred-dollar bill from my dad falls out of my little key pocket. It seems like bad luck, so instead of putting it back in, I leave it as a bookmark in Zena's *Us* magazine.

Once outside, I crouch down to get my backpack from under the bush. When I stand up and glance back at the motel, I see my uncle peering out through the lobby window. Why do I have to see my uncle watching me leave? He's up early for the breakfast buffet, reading the newspaper, and I wave, and he looks at me like he's onto me. But I can outrun him, so it's okay.

He gives me a little wave and I hide the bag on my other shoulder, then start running.

I run under a banner that says KEYSTONE KEY TO THE BLACK HILLS MARATHON. A car goes by and some older guys leer out the window.

I run to the gas station where I told Andre to meet me—I'd scoped it out when my grandpa and I went running before dinner.

I think about that first day of our trip when I rushed into the gas station convenience store after Zena, and how that guy with the twirled mustache wanted to talk to her. Now here I am. Totally twelvulnerable, like her.

Tip: Never run away when you're wearing short shorts.

I pace around the parking lot nervously, feeling kind of stupid, but also determined.

Andre shows up to meet me, panting and out of breath. "I think Lee saw me," he says, and we both start laughing. "This should be a good place to catch a ride. Any prospects yet?"

"No. Did you make a sign?" I ask.

"A sign?" His forehead creases in confusion.

"You know, a sign. Like, 'L.A. or Bust,'" I explain. "Or whatever. We're hitching, right?"

"Yes, but subtly, so we don't get caught," Andre says. "Are you new at this?"

"Like you're not," I tell him. "You brought a big enough bag."

"I'm not planning to come back for a while," he says. "Hey, check it out. Here comes our ride."

A dated-looking avocado-colored RV with Ohio license plates pulls into the gas station. The RV is about as long as a football field and takes up two pump islands.

"Well, at least there would be room for your bag in there," I tease him.

"Shut up. Come on, let's ask them for a ride," Andre says.

"We'll have to see who's driving first," I say. "Check them out before they check *us* out."

"You think anyone dangerous gets around in *that* thing?" Andre asks.

We watch as a family with parents, a couple sets of grandparents, and six kids piles out of the RV.

"Told you," Andre says. "Come on, that's our ticket."

"We're here, kids! We did it!" The dad starts to high-five all the assorted kids as they all run around the RV, like some bizarre exercise/travel routine.

"Reginald. We're not *all* the way there," one of the grandparents says.

"Mother, please. This is as close as it gets without being able to actually touch Mount Rushmore. You said you needed to stretch your legs, so do it. I'll top off the tank."

"So we're actually doing this?" Andre asks as we walk over to the RV. Since the vehicle is so huge, it's not a long walk. "Ditching. Bolting. Abandoning ship."

I laugh. "I should have known not to worry. Your vocabulary can get us out of any dangerous situations."

Andre narrows his eyes. "What dangerous situations?"

"I don't know. Two teenagers with luggage. Doesn't exactly look, um . . ."

"Copacetic."

"Right."

"Or logical," says Andre. "But let's see if they'll give us a ride." We walk over and introduce ourselves, mention that we're headed back home to California, that our car broke down and we have no way to get there.

"Really," the dad, Reginald, says. "You two don't look old enough to be out here on your own."

"Oh, we're young, but we're in college," Andre says. "I'm eighteen and so is she."

"We took lots of AP courses," I add, which sounds really stupid.

"We actually were here on, uh, a class project," Andre says. "Extra-credit summer course. Exploring the great back roads of America."

"And you're students at . . . ?" the wife asks.

"USC," Andre says quickly.

"Great school. Great football team. Nothing like Ohio State, of course." Reginald grins and half punches Andre's shoulder.

"Gotta love the Buckeyes," Andre says, nodding.

"Did we mention we'd give you some money for gas?" I add out of nowhere, smiling at the mom.

"We could take you as far as Denver," Reginald offers.

"Denver would be . . . incredible," Andre says, shaking his hand. "Thank you, sir. You have no idea how much this helps."

"A couple of road rules," his wife says after we meet the kids and grandparents, and we all step into the RV. "One, no smoking. Two, no anything else."

I nod. "Got it."

We try to find room to sit down and end up crammed onto a small bench together, facing the six kids on a sofa opposite us, grandparents on either side of us in seats. We pull out onto the road, but it's slow going. There's tons of traffic because of the marathon, which starts at eight. Streets are blocked off. We're moving so slowly that I glance out the window, wondering if I'll see my grandfather running—and passing us.

"This reminds me of a bus trip I took once," Andre says, smiling.

"Oh, I love bus trips," one of the grandfathers says.

One of the boys keeps sticking out his tongue at me, while another is making arm farts. The two girls are playing one of those clap-and-sing things that drive me crazy, and there's another boy in Spider-Man one-piece PJs, who's got his arms folded in front of him and is just staring at me. He looks about five years too old for Spider-Man PJs.

"Is this a great plan or what?" Andre asks out of the side of his mouth.

"No," I say as the camper struggles up its first hill. "Probably not."

"Well, you know what they say," the dad calls over his shoulder from the driver's seat. "You can't rush Mount Rushmore!"

Andre and I look at each other. It's like that movie *Groundhog Day*. We'll wake up every morning and go to Mount Rushmore until we change our ways.

One of the grandmothers falls asleep and, after a few minutes, rests her head on my shoulder. The other one is firing off questions at Andre, who's trying to answer them as best as he can, while he now has two of the boys in his face, attempting to arm-wrestle with him.

We go slower and slower. The engine groans. I glance out the window to see if we're actually moving at all, and I see black exhaust—or smoke—coming out from underneath the RV.

Finally Reginald pulls over, or attempts to. "Kids—folks—every-body off!" he says. "The Check Engine light is on. I'm going to refill the coolant, see if that takes care of the problem."

"Haven't we been on this bus before?" I ask Andre as we get out and stand by the side of the road—well, what's left of it, with the giant field-size vehicle pulled over. I don't know who looks or feels more pathetic—me, him, or the avocado RV.

Or maybe the boy in the Spider-Man PJs, who now has to watch dozens of cars and hundreds of people pass by, in his footed pajamas.

"Is it us, do you think? Are we a curse?" I ask Andre as Reginald works on the RV. People are honking their car horns because they have to go out into the oncoming lane to get around the giant beached whale of a camper. I think about Grandpa saying to Lenny, "You should have gone around," and if these cars don't go around, they'll probably overheat, too, and this town will grind to a halt, filled with broken-down automobiles.

"You want to kill time by writing some postcards?" Andre asks me.

"Not really," I say. I stretch my arms over my head and wonder if Mom and Zena are awake yet, if they've noticed that I'm gone and wondered where I am. "You want to learn some vocab?"

Andre shrugs. "Not particularly. And just so you know, you have ink on your stomach," he tells me.

"Really?"

"Yeah." He reaches out to show me where, and I flinch at his touch, then laugh, embarrassed.

"Oh yeah. I put a postcard there earlier," I say. "I forgot about it."

"You carry postcards on your lean little tummy. Okay." He leans forward to try to make out the words on my stomach. "Right. Okay, so, let's say this RV doesn't make it another foot. How much money do you have?"

"About forty bucks."

"What happened to the hundred?"

"I left it with my sister," I say.

Andre stares at me as if I'm the dumbest person on the planet. "Okay, who gives away a hundred bucks and then decides to run away? Who does that? Talk about a bad plan. You're undercutting yourself. Sabotaging. Derailing."

"Probably," I admit. "But I didn't want to use it. It seemed unlucky, since it came from my dad."

"For what it's worth," Andre says, "he seemed like a nice enough guy."

"He is. Or he was. He's just . . . pretty screwed up right now."

"Yeah. He seemed a little on edge. But not like terminal. Hopeless. A lost cause," says Andre.

"No? Really?" I ask.

Andre shakes his head. "You want a definition of that? You can check out *my* dad."

"But your dad's good to you."

"Sure, yeah. But he's also never going to be a big part of my life," Andre says. "I kind of realized that when I met his eighteenth girlfriend over the phone last week when I called. He spent about two minutes talking to me; then he had to go."

"Well, what did he say when you told him you were coming?" I ask.

"I didn't exactly tell him yet," Andre says. "If I called to tell him, he'd call my mom to alert her, and we'd never have gotten out the door."

"So . . . did you leave her a note?" I ask.

"Sure, of course. I put it in Cuddles's food dish. I know she'll look there," Andre says.

"What if Cuddles eats the note first?" I ask.

"Hm. I didn't think of that."

"He does like to eat paper. Pop-Tarts boxes, anyway," I remind him.

"Well, I wrote it on an actual Pop-Tart, so it should be safe," Andre jokes.

All this talk about Pop-Tarts makes me realize how hungry I am, so I reach into my bag, searching for an energy or granola bar. I usually take some extras from the continental breakfasts and stash them in my backpack. Instead of finding one, though, my fingers close around a plastic case I don't recognize, so I pull it out to see what it is.

I start smiling, then laughing. "Look." I hold up the *Oklahoma!* CD.

"Oh, man, you actually stole it?" Andre asks.

"I didn't. Didn't you?"

He shakes his head.

"Then . . . who?" But I think I know the answer to that already. The only other person we talked about this with was Grandpa. He didn't tell me that he'd taken it. He just left it for me to find. "When did he do that?" I wonder out loud.

I turn the case over in my hands, tracing the scratches in the case. The CD is so worn that it's amazing it still works. Did he want me to throw it out, I wonder, or keep it as a memento?

Either way, he's onto me, I can't help thinking. He knows I'm leaving and this is his attempt to get me back. And I hate him and I love him for it.

"You know what?" I turn to Andre and take his hands. "I think you're, like . . . the coolest person I've ever known. That I'll ever know, period."

"I feel the same about you. Otherwise I wouldn't be out here getting carbon monoxide poisoning." He waves his hand in front of his face as Reginald restarts the RV and a cloud of black smoke kicks out.

"But I still can't do this," I go on, as difficult as it is.

"You can't? Why not?"

"Because . . . this will sound really rude. Mean. Thoughtless."

"You're doing the three synonyms thing," he says.

"Oh. Sorry." I think of how much I'll miss that, how I'll probably keep doing that all year, and nobody will understand why, or that it's cool and in honor of Andre. "It's just . . . I really love spending time with you, and there's nothing more I want to do than get off that bus and away from my family for even one night. It's, like, *such* a great fantasy."

"So what's the problem?" he asks.

I think about our dysfunctional family dinner the night before. "The past year has been really hard. We've sort of had enough drama. If I take off, I'll be a little too much like my dad. He's never there anymore. Not even when he had the chance, the possibility, of taking off with me and Zena. He didn't show up. And even though my mom is not cool at all, I think I'd better not take off, too."

Andre looks at me and slides his sunglass visors up so he can get a better look. "You're serious. We've come this far. We've got a ride. And you want to go back."

"You know how nuts your mom went when Cuddles ran off? What do you think she'd do if you go missing?"

"I'm no Cuddles. I don't compete," he says.

"Shut up already. You're her favorite boy."

"No, I'm her *only* boy."

"Same thing," I say.

"Andre? Ariel? We're good to go," Reginald tells us. "Come on back in!"

He waves, then climbs back behind the driver's seat. His wife steps up into the passenger seat, the kids and grandparents clamber in, and Andre and I just stand there beside the road, not yet moving.

Reginald honks the horn, which sounds like an injured—or mating—moose must sound. The mom leans out the front window. "Kids, you coming?"

Andre narrows his eyes at her. "Did she just call us kids? Okay, I am definitely not going now." He picks up his backpack and waves at her. "We're good! Thanks!"

"You sure?"

"Yes, thanks anyway!" I call to her. "Have fun at Rushmore!"

"Good luck!" she calls back.

All the kids press their faces to the windows. One boy sticks his tongue out at me, and the two girls give us beauty-queen waves, while Spider-Man boy glares, and then gives us the finger.

"Well. We might have problems, but at least we're not in *that* family," Andre comments as they inch up the hill away from us. "Freaks."

"Totally," I agree. "So. You want to go out to breakfast or something?"

"Sure."

We walk and walk down the hill, into town, until we find a diner and sit down at a booth. I open the menu, wanting to order something big and hearty like an omelet and pancakes, except here they're called "flapjacks," which makes me laugh so hard that Andre nearly calls for a defibrillator.

"Flapjack," I explain. "It's like . . ." I find that I can't explain it, but I'll have to just buy a postcard of the place, so that I remember.

I meet Uncle Jeff at the fun run start line at noon, while Andre heads to the finish line.

"Ariel!" Uncle Jeff says when he sees me approaching. "You scared us half to death. Where on earth did you go?"

"Andre and I went on a, uh, hike. My dad's not around by any chance, is he?" I ask, eager to change the subject of Andre when Uncle Jeff is around, for obvious reasons. It's not every day your uncle sees you making out with a guy on the ground. And it shouldn't be.

Uncle Jeff shrugs. "Haven't seen him."

"Huh." I'm not surprised, but I wish the news were different. I stretch my muscles and look for a place to stash my backpack so it'll be safe. I decide to just wear it, so I don't lose anything. "Hey, Uncle Jeff. Do you ever read people's postcards?" I ask as we count down the last minute before the run.

"Oh no, of course not, that would be unethical," Uncle Jeff says, as if he's never done anything unethical, like, for instance, try to kill an innocent squirrel. "Anyway, I don't look at every individual piece of mail; it's in a presorted stack. On the other hand, if it looks interesting and I want to know what the picture is, I look at the back, and sometimes, well . . ."

"You can't help but read it," I say.

"Maybe. But usually I don't have time, and to be honest I don't care," he says. "Postcards are short and usually boring. Where it gets interesting is certified mail." He bends down, stretching his hamstrings. "So, how do you think I'll do?"

"You'll do great," I say. "You've trained and you're ready. Pretty much. Plus it's a fun run, so it's not exactly like a race, you know?"

"But I have one question. What's fun about running when it's a hundred degrees?"

I smile. "Feeling the accomplishment. The sweat. The journey." I shrug. "Things of that nature."

"Exactamundo," Uncle Jeff says. And he laughs. "Don't you hate it when Lenny says that all the time?"

"Hey, you got sneakers," I say, pointing at his feet. "When did you get those?"

"Last night. What do you think of them?"

"Well, the most important thing is, how do they feel?"

He twirls his right foot in a circle. "They feel fantastic, but what do I know?"

"Fantasterrific," I correct him.

Uncle Jeff looks at me like he's never heard that word before. As if I'm making it up or something.

"They look great," I say instead.

"I think so too," he says.

As we line up and start running along the course, I notice my grandmother in a bright lilac tracksuit holding up a big sign that says, GO, ARIEL!

We go a little farther and I see Mom in her new Mount Rushmore T-shirt, and I don't know if I should tell her that a woman as big as she is shouldn't wear a T-shirt with mountains printed over her breasts.

And if she does, she definitely shouldn't jump up and down and cheer.

Grandpa's at the finish line, waiting for us. He congratulates Uncle Jeff, but for once he doesn't look happy to see me. "Where were you? I had to run the half marathon alone." He glances over at Andre, who's nearby in the crowd, headed our way, and doesn't look thrilled to see him, either. Andre takes the hint and veers off toward the Gatorade tent.

"You survived okay?" I ask.

"Sure. But there was no one to talk to or help pace me. Just a bunch of young idiots obsessed with their splits," he complains.

"How'd you do?"

He frowns. "Second in my age group. Some ringer from Sioux Falls beat me. So. You still leaving?" he asks. "Or did you just come back to say good-bye?" He's hurt, and I'm surprised that he shows it.

I pull out the *Oklahoma!* CD. "How did you know that was my bag, and why it was outside?"

"As I think I've said before, being head of this family is a full-time job. I was out for an early-morning run, of course. A warm-up. I saw it sitting on the balcony. I figured you were up to something."

"So how did you get this?" I ask him.

He slips on his warm-up jacket. "I have ways."

He's not a hugger, but I hug him anyway. He doesn't seem to mind, but his body doesn't give, either; it's kind of like hugging a surfboard.

Grandpa pats my shoulder. "Here comes Lenny. For God's sake, put away that CD, or it'll be 'Oh, What a Beautiful Mornin'" all the way back to Sioux Falls. And by the way? You owe me a half marathon."

Mom's waiting for me when I get back to the motel to change. She's sitting on the bed with a notebook, writing.

"You probably have something to tell me," I say as I close the door behind me. I toss my backpack onto the bed and go over to my suitcase to get out some clean clothes. I can't wait to take a shower.

"Actually, that's what *I* was going to say. What happened to you?" Mom asks.

I turn to face her. "Should I tell you everything, or just the important stuff?"

"Tell me everything," she says sternly. "I'll decide what's important."

I sigh. "Would you settle for the Clairol highlights?"

"Okay." She closes the notebook and sets it on the bedside table.

I sink down on the bed beside her. "Andre and I went out for breakfast and a walk. I figured out some stuff. Here I am."

She watches me carefully, trying to interpret my condensed version of things. "That's it?"

I think about the last few hours. Someday I'll tell her all the details, and it'll be hilarious, but not now. "We also rode in an RV for about twelve feet. With a huge family and a bunch of obnoxious kids."

She nods, considering whether that's a felony or not. "Is *that* it?" she asks.

"Yup. Oh, and some guys in a car tried to hit on me. It was a drive-by type thing."

She lets out her breath and runs her hand through her brown-gray-blond hair. "I can't *wait* for this trip to be over."

I smile, amused by the turn of events. "So, what happened with Dad? Did he ever show up?"

"Not exactly," she says. "This was taped to our room door this morning when we headed out for the day." She reaches into the notebook and pulls out a postcard. "Go ahead; read it."

"We hold these truths to be self-evident, that all men are created equal, that they are endowed by their Creator with certain unalienable rights, that among these are Life, Liberty, and the Pursuit of Happiness."
—One of the granite giants of Mount Rushmore, Thomas Jefferson (second from left)

Tamara, Ariel, & Zena,

It was great to see you guys. Sorry I had to take off, but things weren't really working out.

I'm sorry I let you guys down. It seems like I can't stop doing that. I'm trying, you know? But not exactly succeeding. Yet.

I hope sometime, like next summer, I'll have things figured out for sure, and we can hit the road (but not the toad) together again.

See you when we all get home.

Love,

Dad

Chapter Twenty-one

Three days later, we stand outside in the Leisure-Lee world headquarters parking lot. Lenny keeps pulling suitcases and bags out of
the bus, like a whale's belly being emptied.

Everyone looks sort of bereft, exhausted, disoriented, like they've
lost something on the road somewhere and they don't know what it
was or when it happened.

Jenny bursts out of the office and runs to Lenny, who hugs her
and twirls her around in the air.

"I knew you'd be here. Happens every time," Lenny explains to
the curious crowd. "Midsummer. We just can't make it."

"It's only June," Zena says out of the corner of her mouth.

Mom gives them her card. "Call me. I do phone sessions."

"Phone sex? You?" Ethel asks.

"*Therapy* sessions, over the phone," Mom explains.

"Oh. I didn't know you could do that."

"What's that?" someone else asks.

"Sex therapy. On the phone," Ethel says.

Mom throws up her hands. "Anyway. If you're interested in growing your relationship, sowing the seeds for future peace and happiness, call me. Heck, I'll send you some of my books for free."

Lenny, Jenny, and Lee say their good-byes and take off for the building to get ready for the next Leisure-Lee adventure. The rest of us are dealing with posttraumatic bus disorder.

My grandfather is sitting on his suitcase, rubbing his calves. "So what do you think? Are you ready for the season?" he asks me.

"Not yet. Not even close," I say. "For one thing, it's going to take another week for my legs to unfurl."

Unfurl? I have got to stop reading Andre's vocabulary book.

"But I've still got two months to be totally ready," I say. "What about you? Going to sign up for another marathon?"

"Maybe. But I think I'm probably going back to work," my grandfather says.

"I think that's probably a good idea," I say, nodding.

"You could tell, huh?"

"I think I'm going back to work too," Uncle Jeff announces. "The vacation days are gone. The holiday's been had. Party's over."

He's doing it too, saying things in threes. We probably all need to be moving on at this point, because we're turning cultish.

"It's like Lee said. If you don't work, you don't get vacation," Uncle Jeff says.

"How profound." Grandma rolls her eyes.

"Maybe you should get a driving route," my grandfather suggests. "You'd have a roof over your head."

Uncle Jeff laughs. "Right. That might be good. But I wouldn't get the exercise I need. Plus I enjoy talking with the people, being out in all kinds of weather, and things of that nature."

My grandmother comes over and stands beside me. "The nice thing is that we don't have to say good-bye. You'll be coming to our house tonight."

"But I really want to see Gloves," I say. "I'm sorry; I hate to admit that."

"She'll be okay. She'll be fine," Grandma says. "But I know what you mean. I really miss our cat, too."

"You do? But you never said anything."

"I don't believe in talking about everything, but it doesn't mean I don't have feelings."

"Right." I smile at her, thinking about her blowup at the restaurant the other night, when everyone melted down.

"Maybe you guys want to split up, ride with us," she suggests.

"Mm, okay," I say. "Well, I don't know. Is that okay with you guys?" I ask Mom and Zena.

"Yes, I get the front seat!" Zena cries, so I guess it's okay with her.

Mom and Zena are hugging Uncle Jeff good-bye, so I walk over to the Coke machine because my throat is parched. Andre comes over to say good-bye. I've been dreading this moment for the past couple of days, and even hoping the second bus would break down so we could spend more time together.

"You're the best person I've ever almost been a runaway with," he begins.

I slide two dollar bills into the pop machine, stand back, and look at my selections. "Is that all you can say?"

"This trip would have been nothing without you. I'd have taken off for sure. Day one. Rest area. Thumbed a ride."

"Been dead by now."

"Exactly," he says.

I choose an orange soda, but when I press the button, the

machine drops a bottle of strawberry milk instead. "What *is* this?" I ask him, turning the bottle over in my hand. "Who even drinks straw-berry milk?"

"I haven't had that since I was two," he says. "Just open it and drink it."

So I have a few sips and hand the bottle to him, and he has a few sips.

"Do you have three words for this?" I ask.

He pauses for a second. "Sucky. Lousy. Pretty much undrinkable."

"Exactly." I stand there, not wanting to leave or say something stupid that he'll remember as my last, stupid words.

"So, like. We should stay in touch," he says.

"We should," I agree.

"And I think I know how. You can send me bad postcards," says Andre.

"Okay," I say, nodding, and then I'm crying. Because I always cry at times like this. It's a yearbook-signing-type moment, saying good-bye. I hate saying good-bye. I don't know what to say, what to write.

My whole life is up in the air, sort of, and unless we move to Chicago instead of St. Paul, I probably won't see Andre much more in my life. I hate thinking that.

"But I don't know about the whole romance thing," Andre says.

"Yeah. Me neither," I say. "I hate to say that. But I guess it seems kind of unrealistic."

"Totally," he agrees.

"Absolutely. Definitely," I add. "Not realistic."

"But since when are we into 'realistic'?" Andre asks. "Anyway, we could visit each other. I think there's this bus tour of Chicago you could take."

"Very funny," I say.

"I thought so. And in the meantime, you know. We're going to have to live on, like, memories. So we'd better have a good Leisure-Lee one to remember." And he kisses me so I back up against the Coke machine and drop the strawberry milk. I hug Andre one last time.

"Come on, Ariel—time to go!" Grandma says, and we break apart, which takes some effort.

Andre and I hold hands until we can't any longer, and then he says, "See you," and wanders across the parking lot to his car.

I turn around to see Bethany and Zena hugging Dieter and Wolfgang, which almost sort of takes something away from my moment, but not quite, because they're never going to have the kind of devastatingly hot kiss Andre and I just had.

Or at least, I hope not, until Zena gets a little older.

When I go over to the car, Grandpa is still trying to fit everything into the trunk. "I can't fit all your shoe boxes into the car, Jeffrey. Did you have to buy so many shoes on the trip? Jeez."

"Did you see how many sweatshirts Tamara bought?" Uncle Jeff points out, as if they're still twelve and ten.

"Yes, but I'm not trying to fit them all in my car," says Grandpa.

"It's genetic. I brought eight pairs myself," I say to Uncle Jeff.

"Really?" Uncle Jeff's eyes light up.

We start to get into the car, but I suddenly remember something I've been meaning to do. "Wait—I almost forgot something. I'll be right back."

I run back to the bus and leave the *Oklahoma!* CD on the steps. I wouldn't want to deprive the next Leisure-Lee guests.

Leisure-Lee Tours: Weekly Departures from Sioux Falls.

When life gives you vacation, take it!

Because when you're driving, you miss the small stuff.

Because you can't rush Mount Rushmore.

Andre,

We're heading home now, or maybe to our new home. Anyway. Crossing Minnesota at the speed of light.

The sky is clear. Cloudless. Beautiful. Azure.

Think of three more and write me back.

I miss you.

But I don't know how much that counts, because at this point, I even miss Lenny.

Pathetically perambulating,

Ariel